W9-BCN-062

# MORE PRAISE FOR BABYMOUSE!

"Sassy, smart . . .
Babymouse is here
to stay."
**—The Horn Book Magazine**

"Young readers
will happily
fall in line."
**—Kirkus Reviews**

"The brother-sister creative team hits the mark
with humor, sweetness, and characters so genuine
they can pass for real kids." **—Booklist**

"Babymouse is spunky, ambitious,
and, at times, a total dweeb."
**—School Library Journal**

Sing your heart out for **all** the **BABYMOUSE** books:

#1 BABYMOUSE: Queen of the World!
#2 BABYMOUSE: Our Hero
#3 BABYMOUSE: Beach Babe
#4 BABYMOUSE: Rock Star
#5 BABYMOUSE: Heartbreaker
#6 CAMP BABYMOUSE
#7 BABYMOUSE: Skater Girl
#8 BABYMOUSE: Puppy Love
#9 BABYMOUSE: Monster Mash
#10 BABYMOUSE: The Musical
#11 BABYMOUSE: Dragonslayer

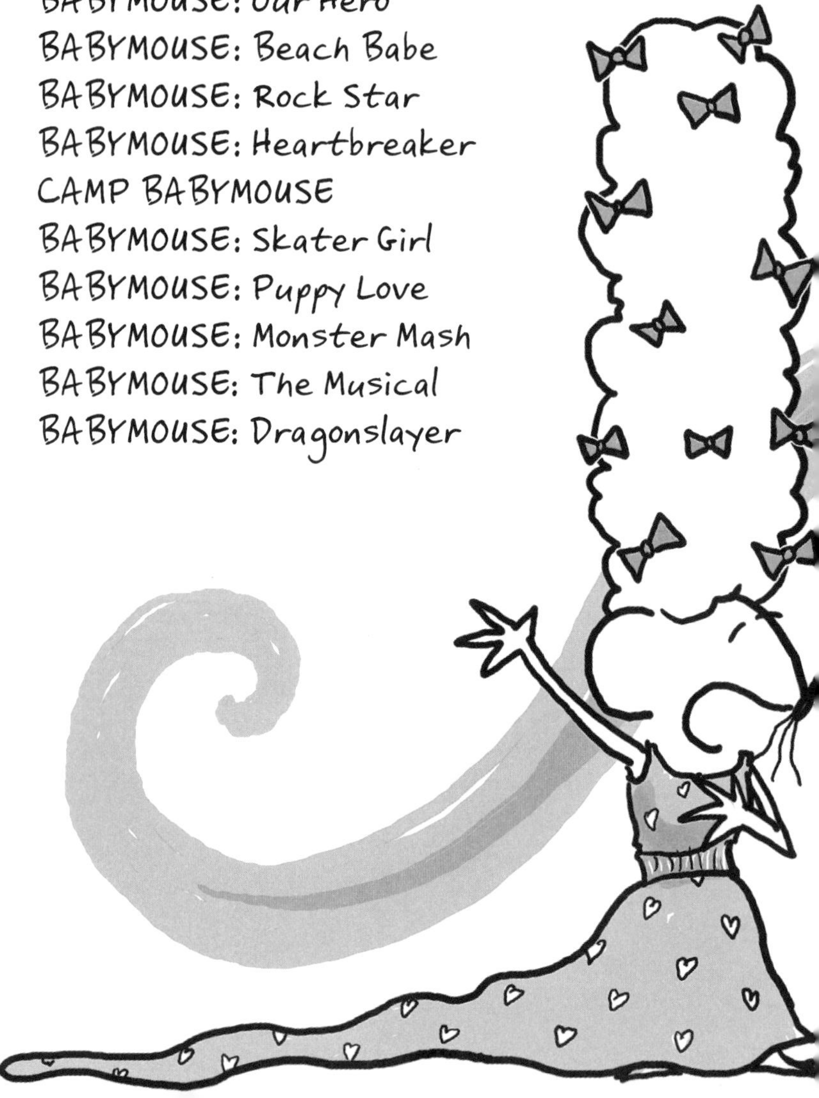

# BABYMOUSE

## THE MUSICAL

## BY JENNIFER L. HOLM & MATTHEW HOLM

RANDOM HOUSE 🏠 NEW YORK

This is a work of fiction. Names, characters, places, and incidents either are the product of the author's imagination or are used fictitiously. Any resemblance to actual persons, living or dead, events, or locales is entirely coincidental.

Copyright © 2009 by Jennifer Holm and Matthew Holm.

All rights reserved.
Published in the United States by Random House Children's Books,
a division of Random House, Inc., New York.

Random House and colophon are registered trademarks of Random House, Inc.

Visit us on the Web!
www.randomhouse.com/kids
www.babymouse.com

Educators and librarians, for a variety of teaching tools, visit us at
www.randomhouse.com/teachers

Library of Congress Cataloging-in-Publication Data
Holm, Jennifer L.
Babymouse : the musical / by Jennifer & Matthew Holm.
   p.   cm.
Summary: As tryouts for the school musical begin, Babymouse takes the starring role
in several imaginary Broadway productions, which also feature her debonair new
classmate, Henry the Hedgehog.
ISBN 978-0-375-84388-4 (trade pbk.) — ISBN 978-0-375-93791-0 (lib. bdg.)
1. Graphic novels. [1. Graphic novels. 2. Musicals—Fiction. 3. Theater—Fiction.
4. Imagination—Fiction. 5. Mice—Fiction. 6. Animals—Fiction. 7. School—Fiction.]
I. Holm, Matthew. II. Title.
PZ7.7.H65Bal 2009 [Fic]—dc22  2008010891

MANUFACTURED IN MALAYSIA  12 11 10 9 8 7

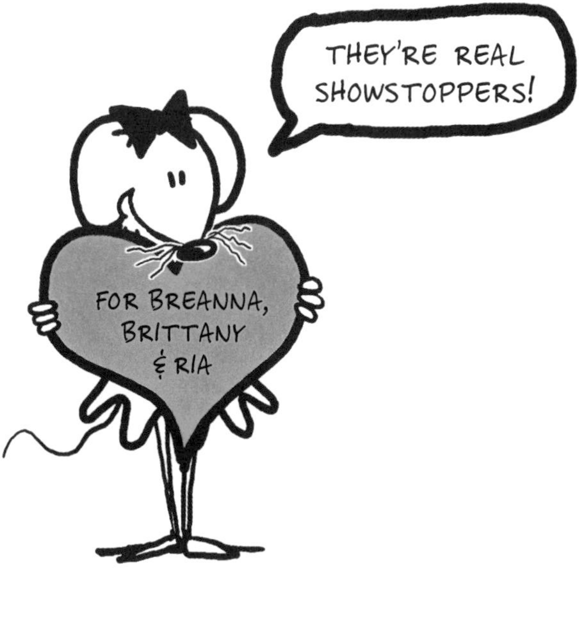
THEY'RE REAL SHOWSTOPPERS!
FOR BREANNA, BRITTANY & RIA

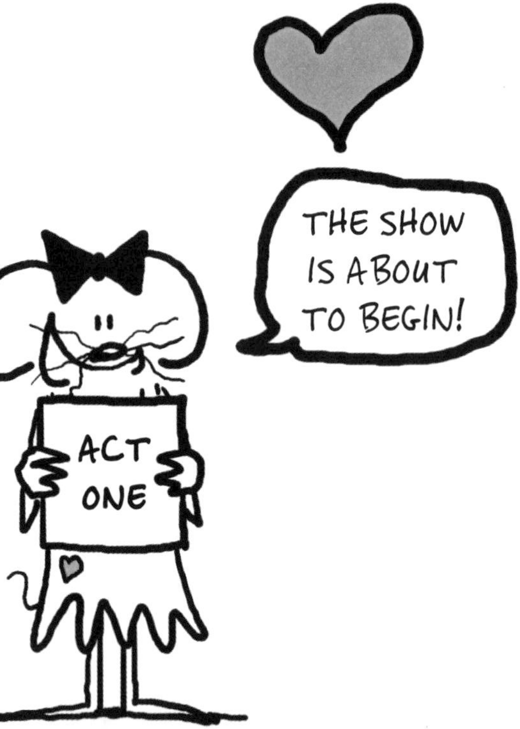
THE SHOW IS ABOUT TO BEGIN!
ACT ONE

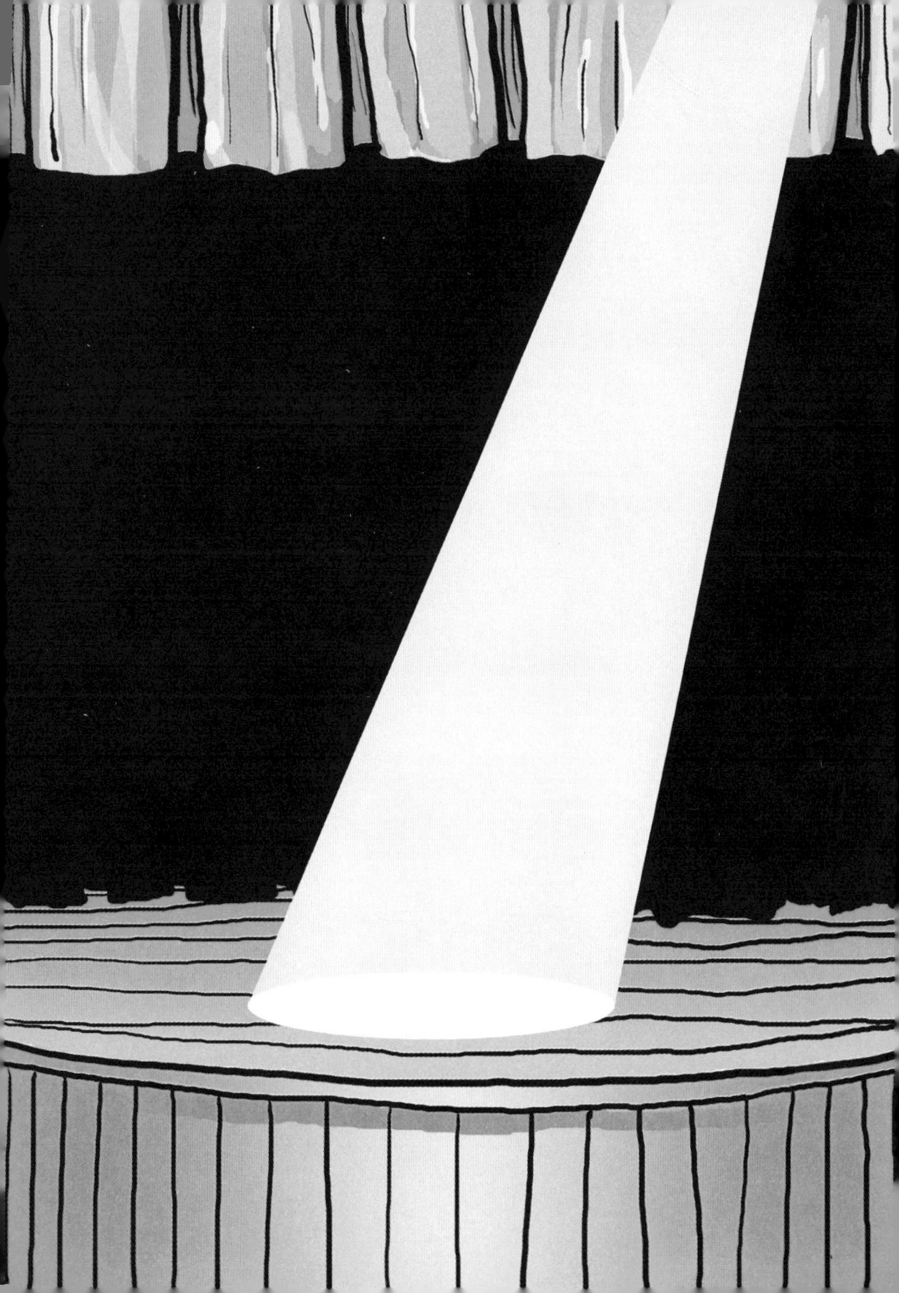

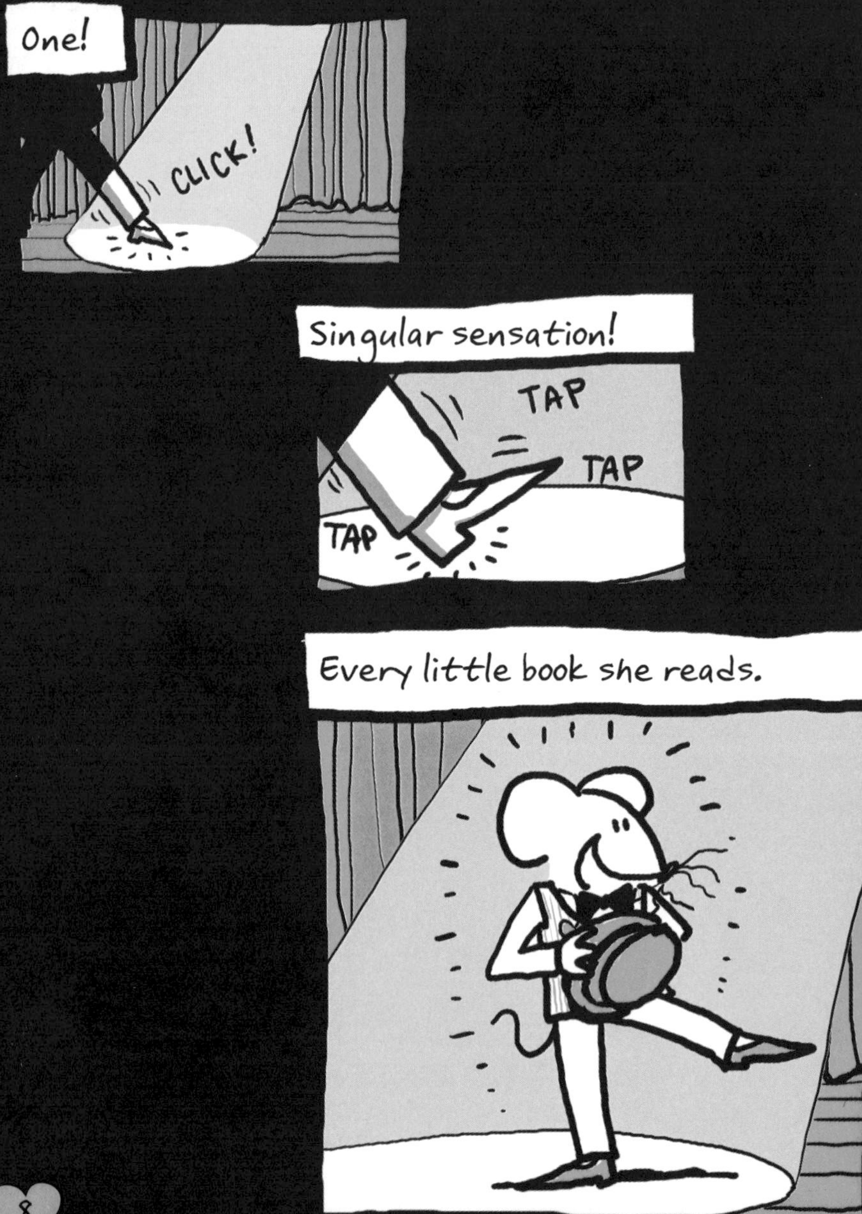

One!
CLICK!
Singular sensation!
TAP
TAP
TAP
Every little book she reads.

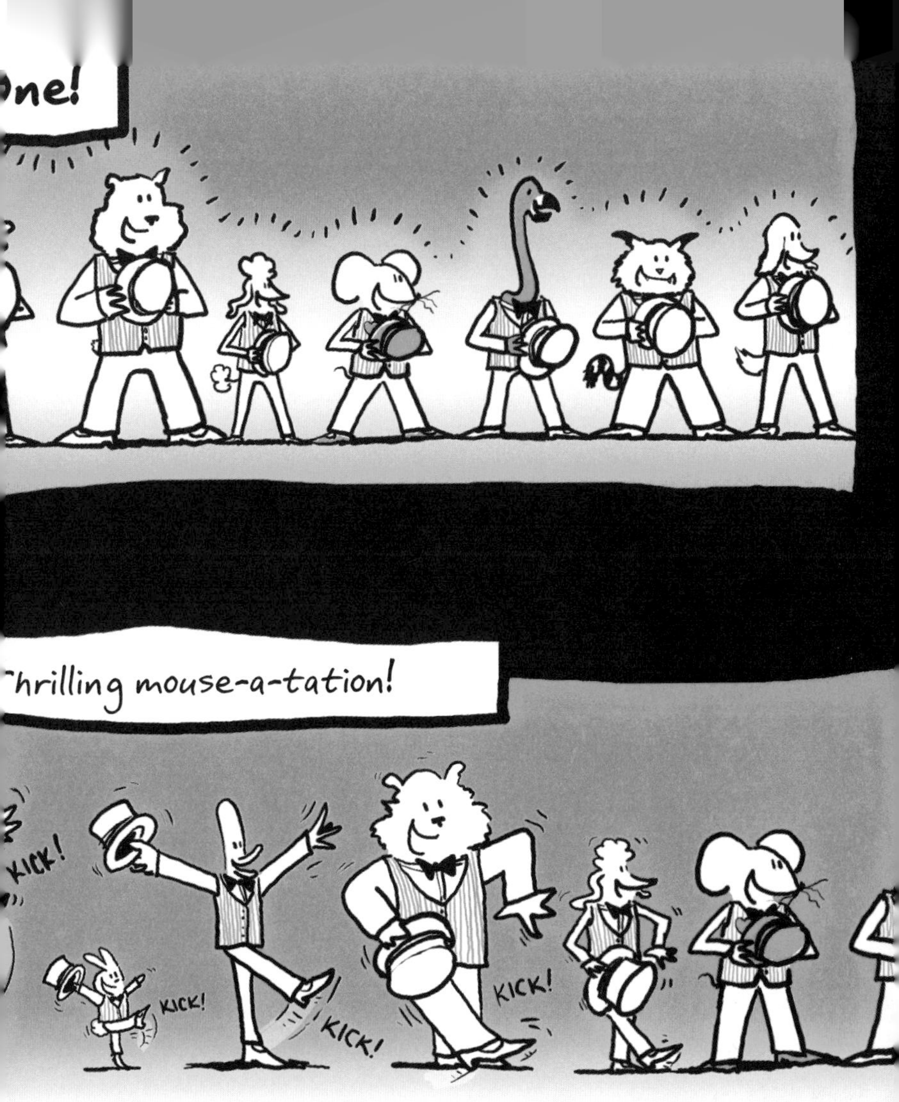

ne!
hrilling mouse-a-tation!
KICK!
KICK!
KICK!
KICK!

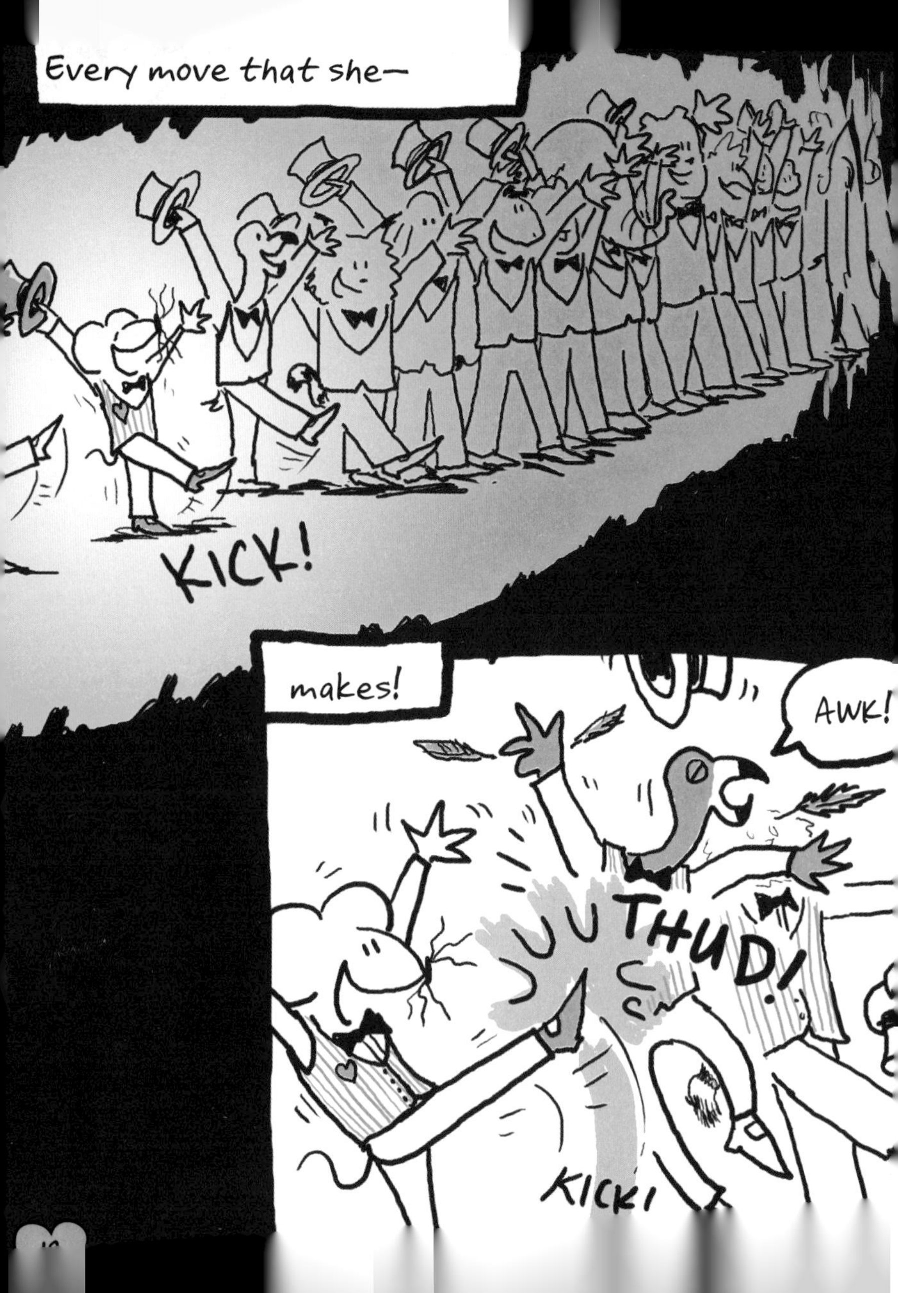
Every move that she—
KICK!
makes!
AWK!
THUD!
KICK!

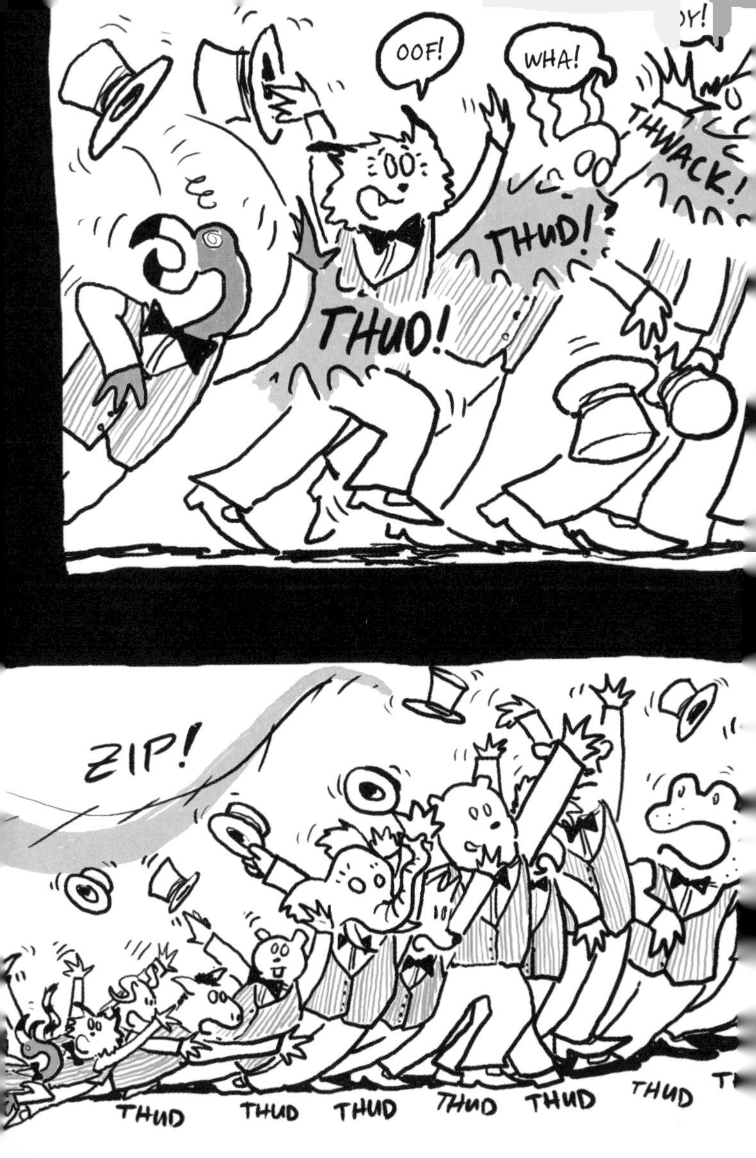

OOF!
WHA!
THWACK!
THUD!
THUD!
ZIP!
THUD
THUD
THUD
THUD
THUD
THUD

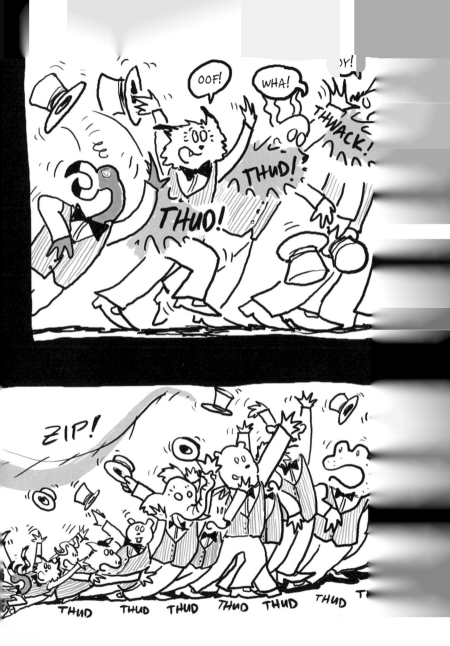

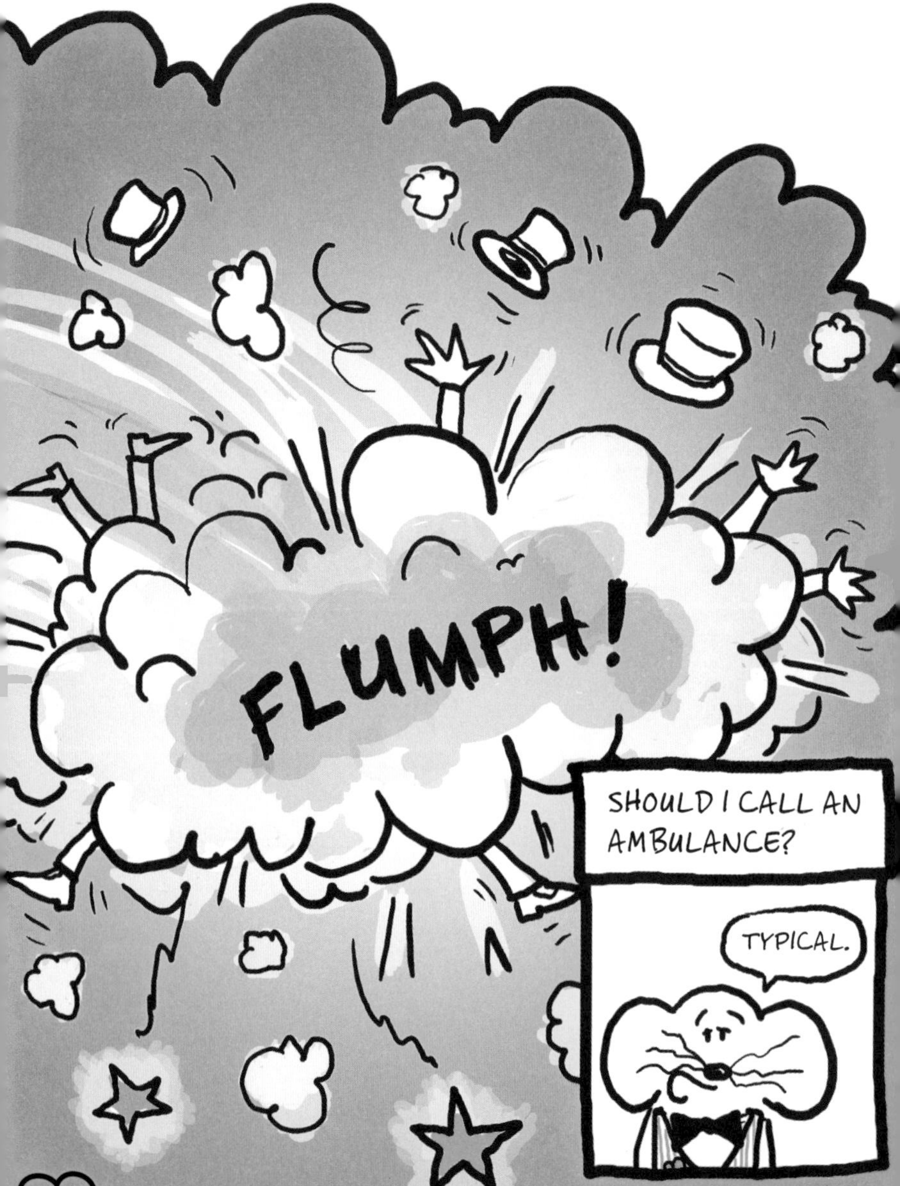

FLUMPH!
SHOULD I CALL AN AMBULANCE?
TYPICAL.

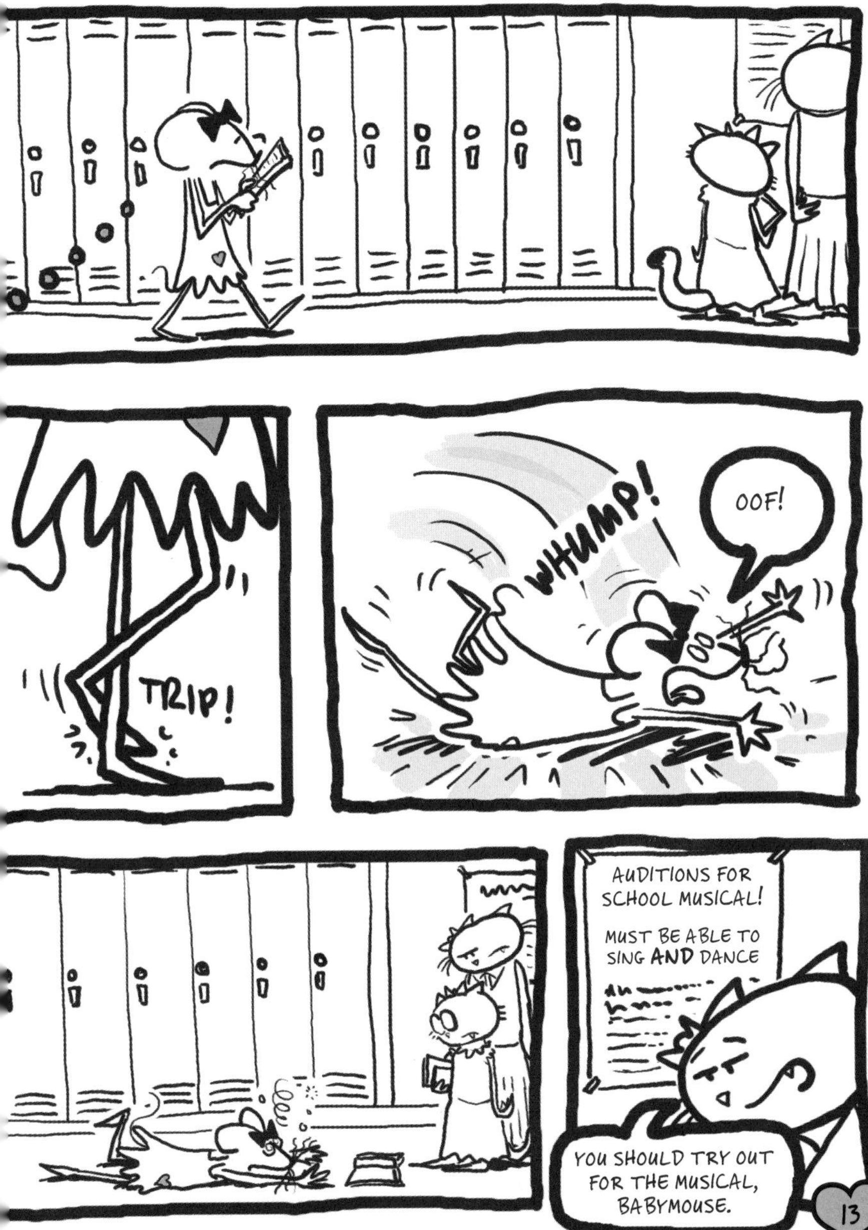
TRIP!
WHUMP!
OOF!
AUDITIONS FOR SCHOOL MUSICAL!
MUST BE ABLE TO SING AND DANCE
YOU SHOULD TRY OUT FOR THE MUSICAL, BABYMOUSE.

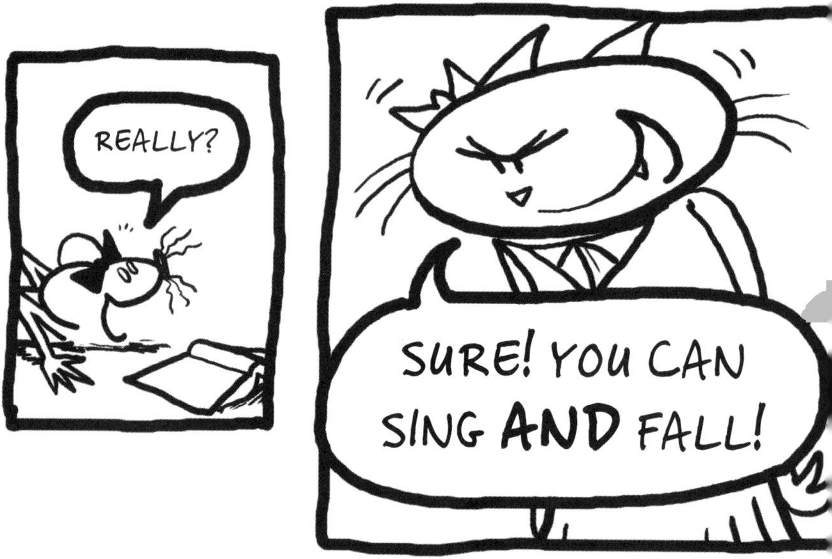
REALLY?
SURE! YOU CAN SING **AND** FALL!

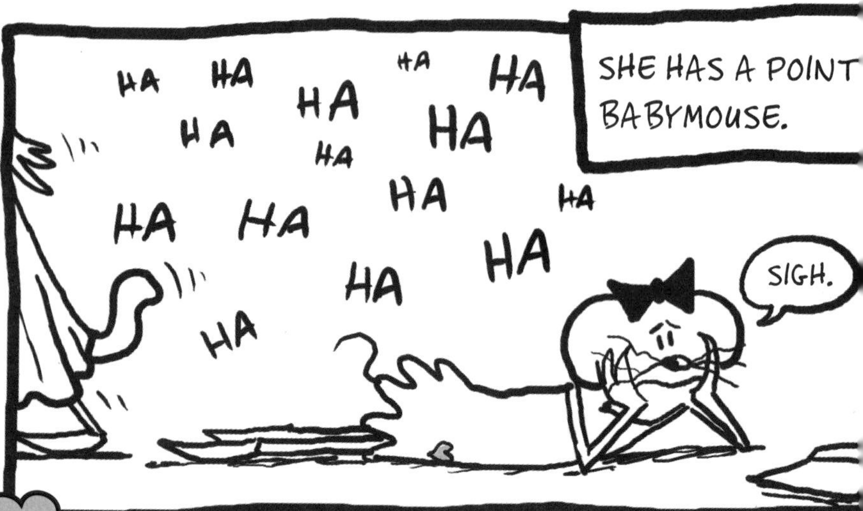
HA HA HA HA HA HA HA HA HA HA HA HA HA HA HA HA HA
SHE HAS A POINT BABYMOUSE.
SIGH.

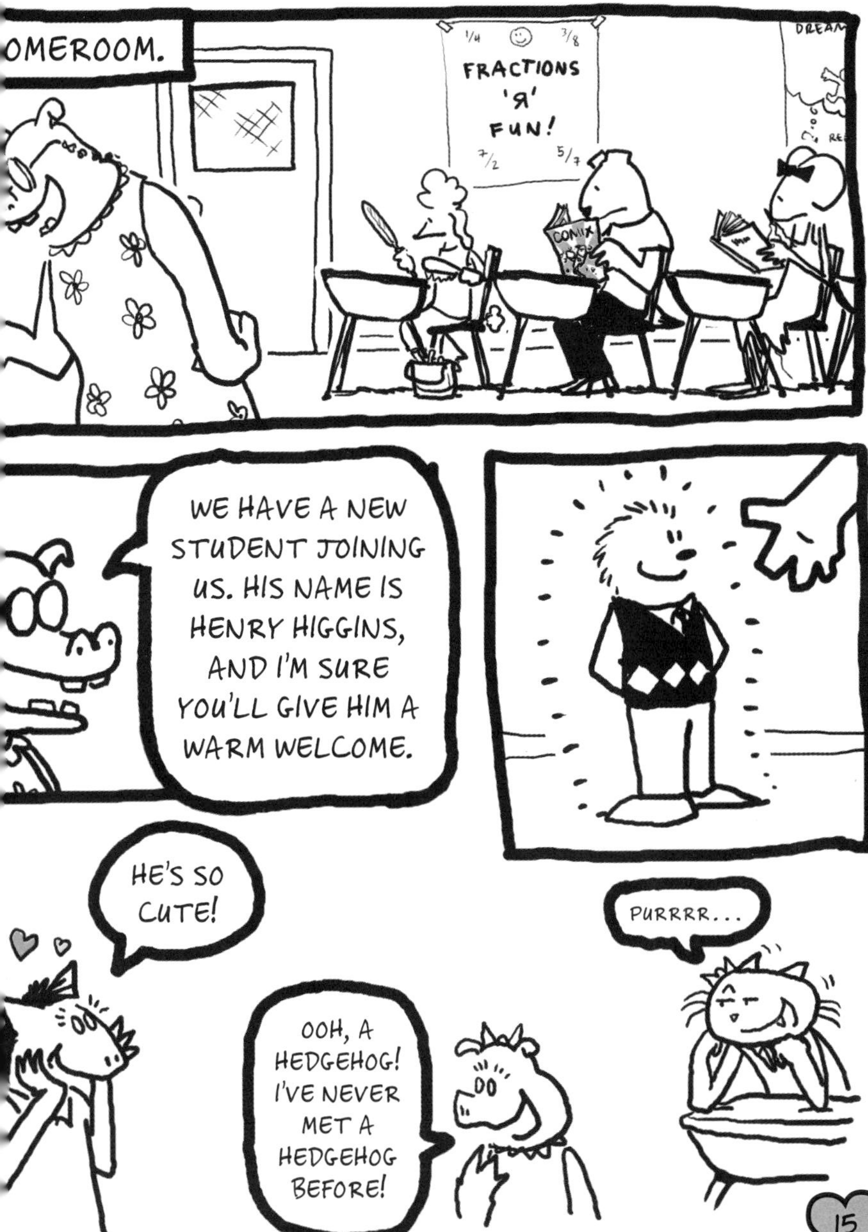

OMEROOM.
1/4 3/8 FRACTIONS 'Я' FUN! 7/2 5/7
COMIX
WE HAVE A NEW STUDENT JOINING US. HIS NAME IS HENRY HIGGINS, AND I'M SURE YOU'LL GIVE HIM A WARM WELCOME.
HE'S SO CUTE!
PURRRR...
OOH, A HEDGEHOG! I'VE NEVER MET A HEDGEHOG BEFORE!

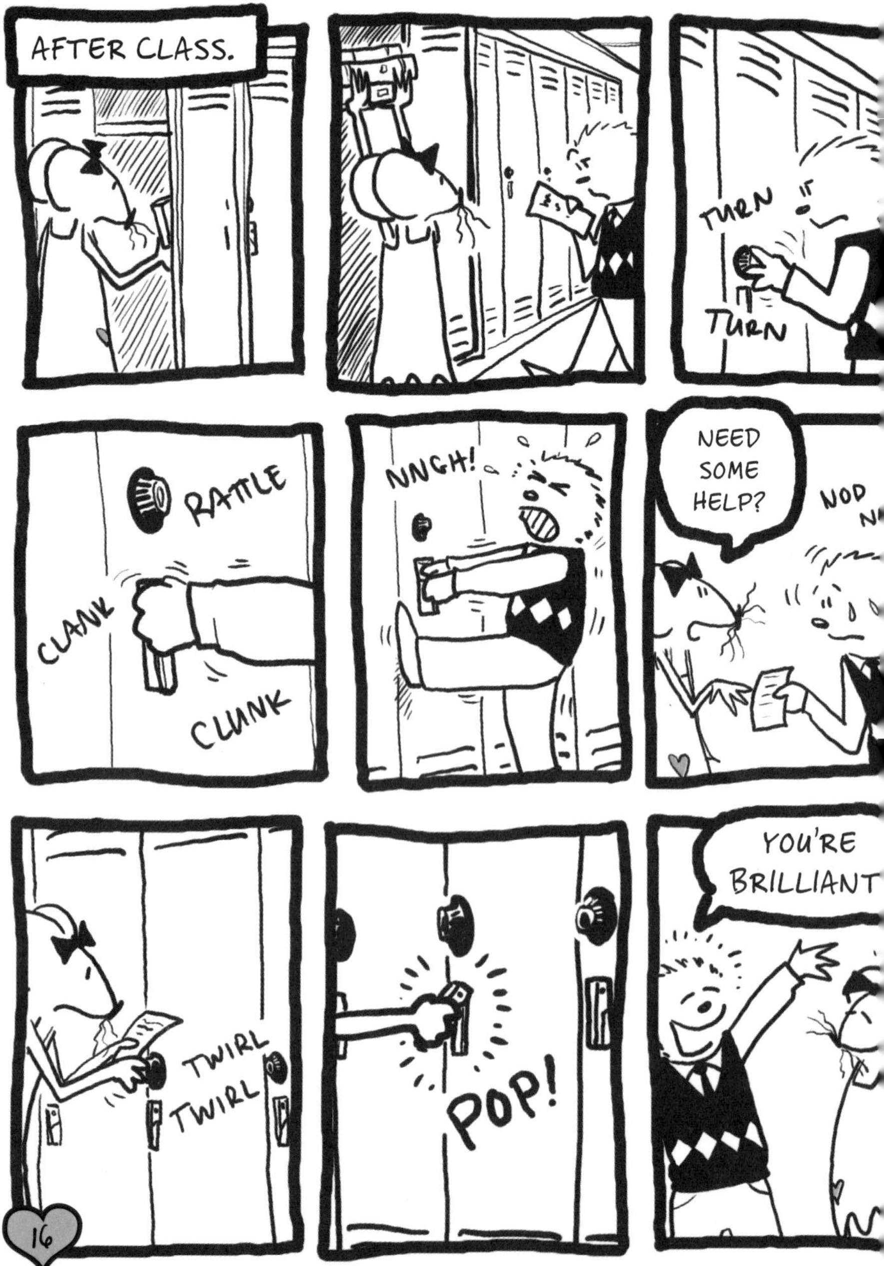
AFTER CLASS.
TURN
TURN
RATTLE
CLANK
CLUNK
NNGH!
NEED SOME HELP?
NOD
TWIRL
TWIRL
POP!
YOU'RE BRILLIANT

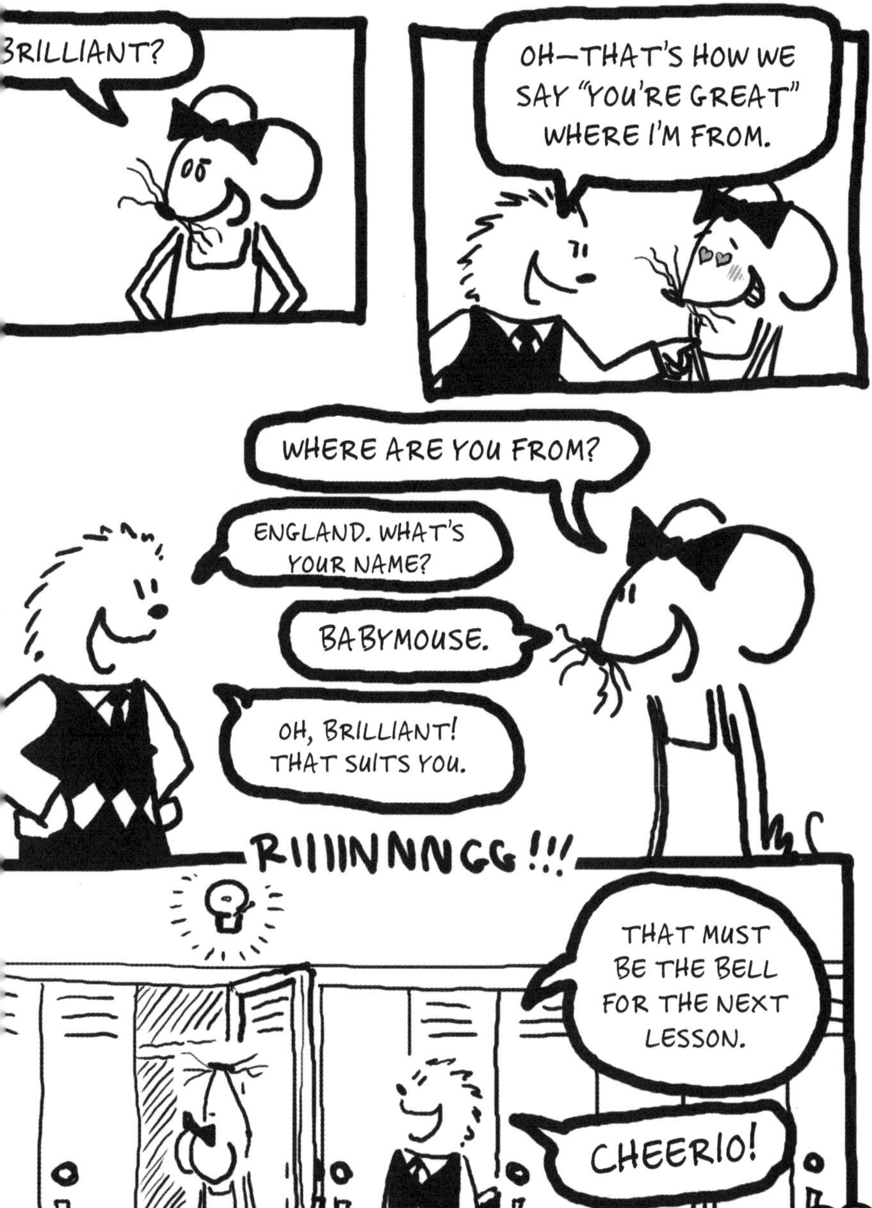
BRILLIANT?
OH—THAT'S HOW WE SAY "YOU'RE GREAT" WHERE I'M FROM.
WHERE ARE YOU FROM?
ENGLAND. WHAT'S YOUR NAME?
BABYMOUSE.
OH, BRILLIANT! THAT SUITS YOU.
RIIIINNNGG!!!
THAT MUST BE THE BELL FOR THE NEXT LESSON.
CHEERIO!

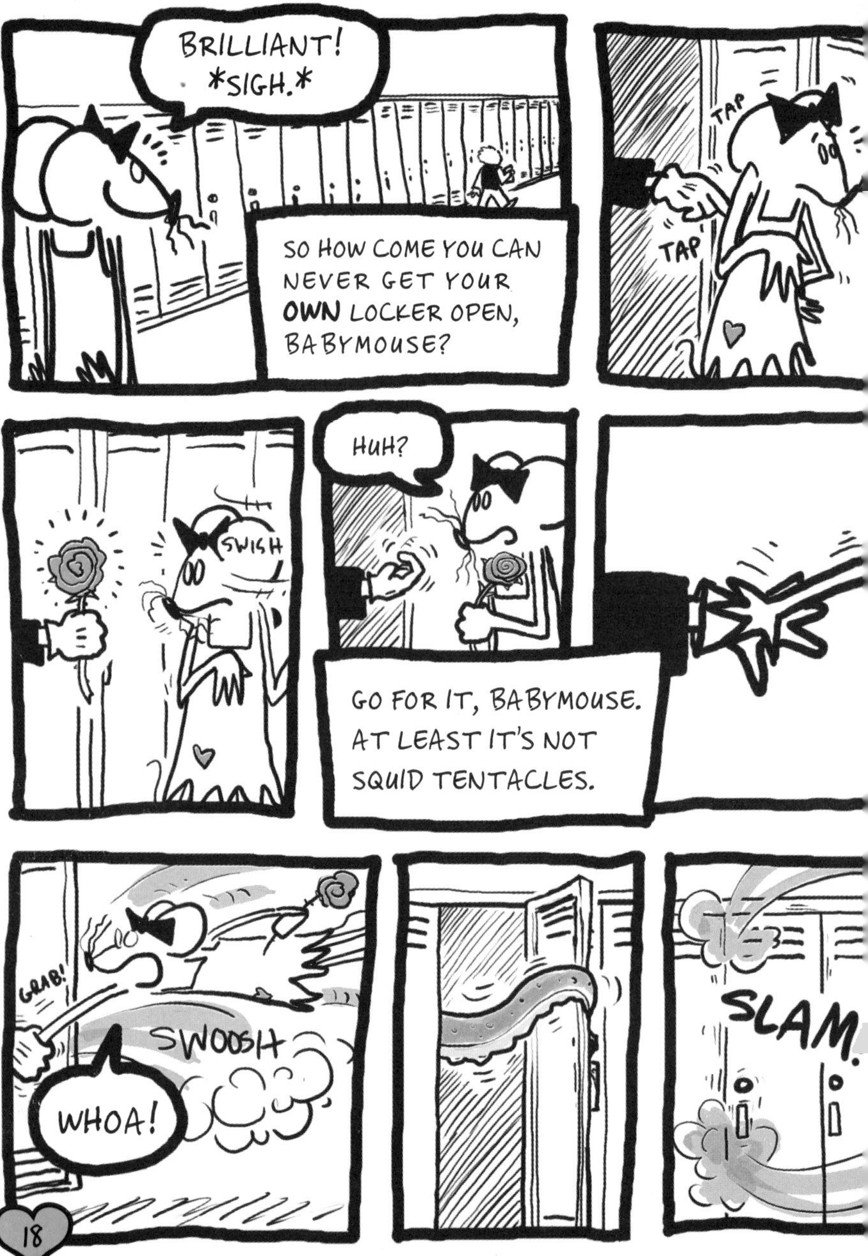
BRILLIANT! *SIGH.*
SO HOW COME YOU CAN NEVER GET YOUR **OWN** LOCKER OPEN, BABYMOUSE?
TAP
TAP
SWISH
HUH?
GO FOR IT, BABYMOUSE. AT LEAST IT'S NOT SQUID TENTACLES.
GRAB!
SWOOSH
WHOA!
SLAM.

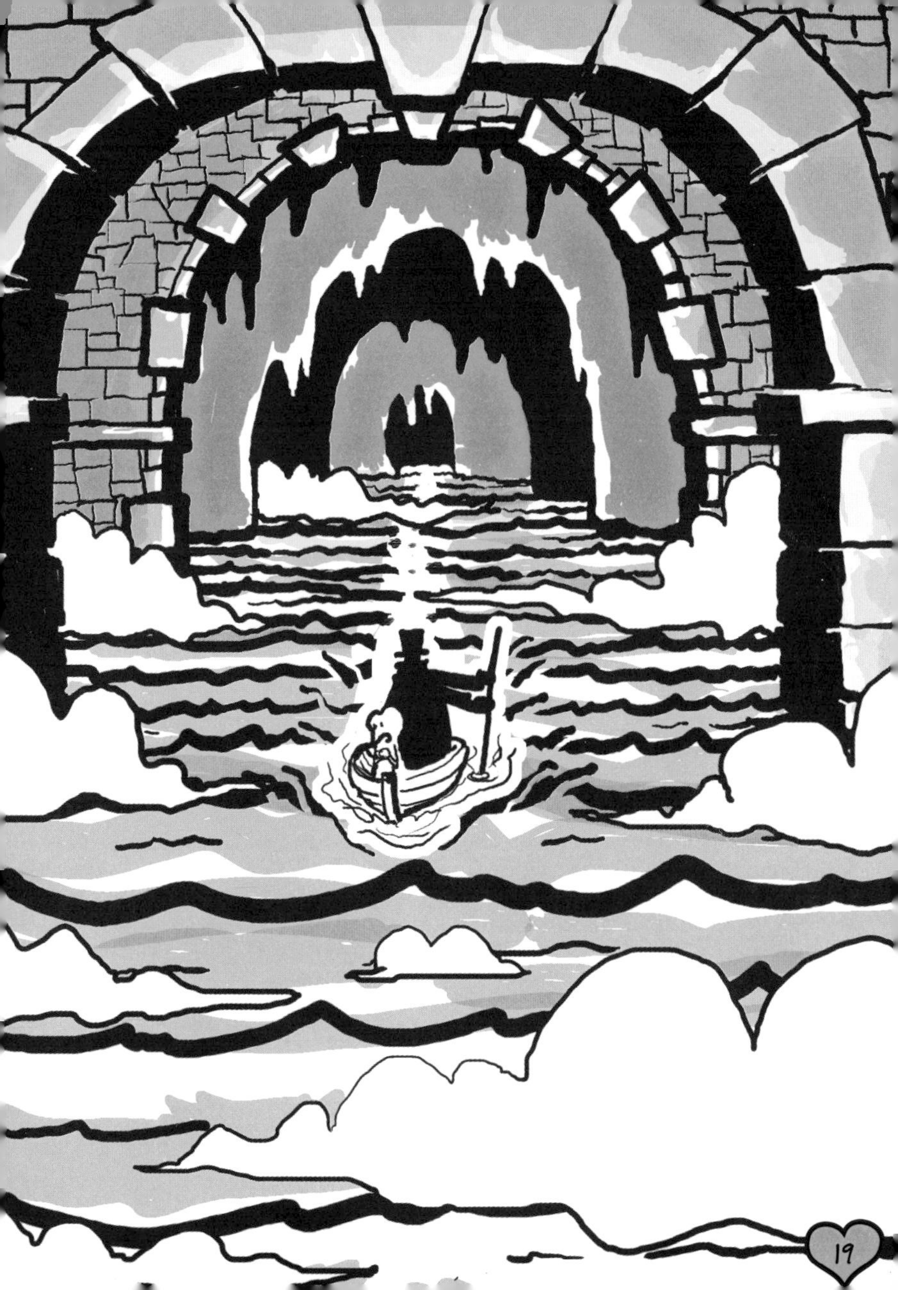

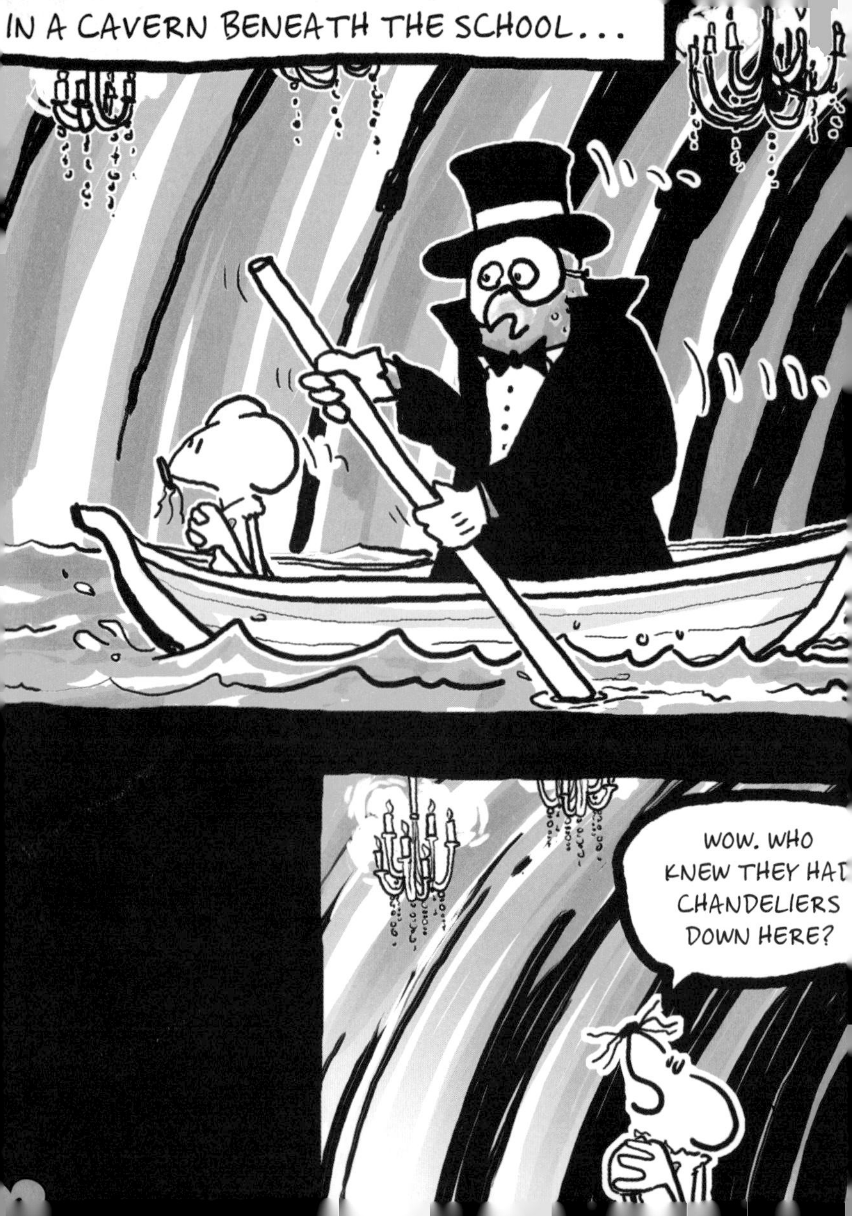
IN A CAVERN BENEATH THE SCHOOL...
WOW. WHO KNEW THEY HAD CHANDELIERS DOWN HERE?

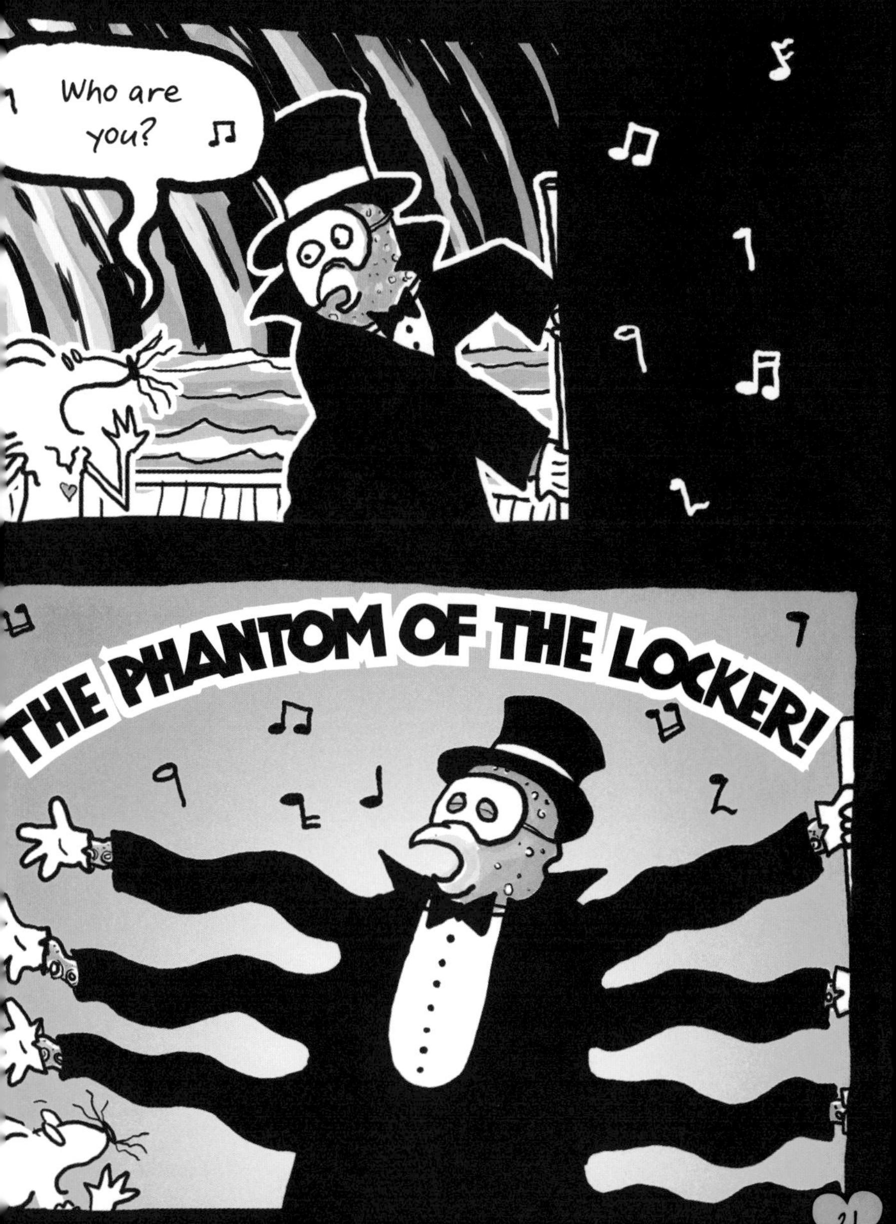
Who are you?
THE PHANTOM OF THE LOCKER!

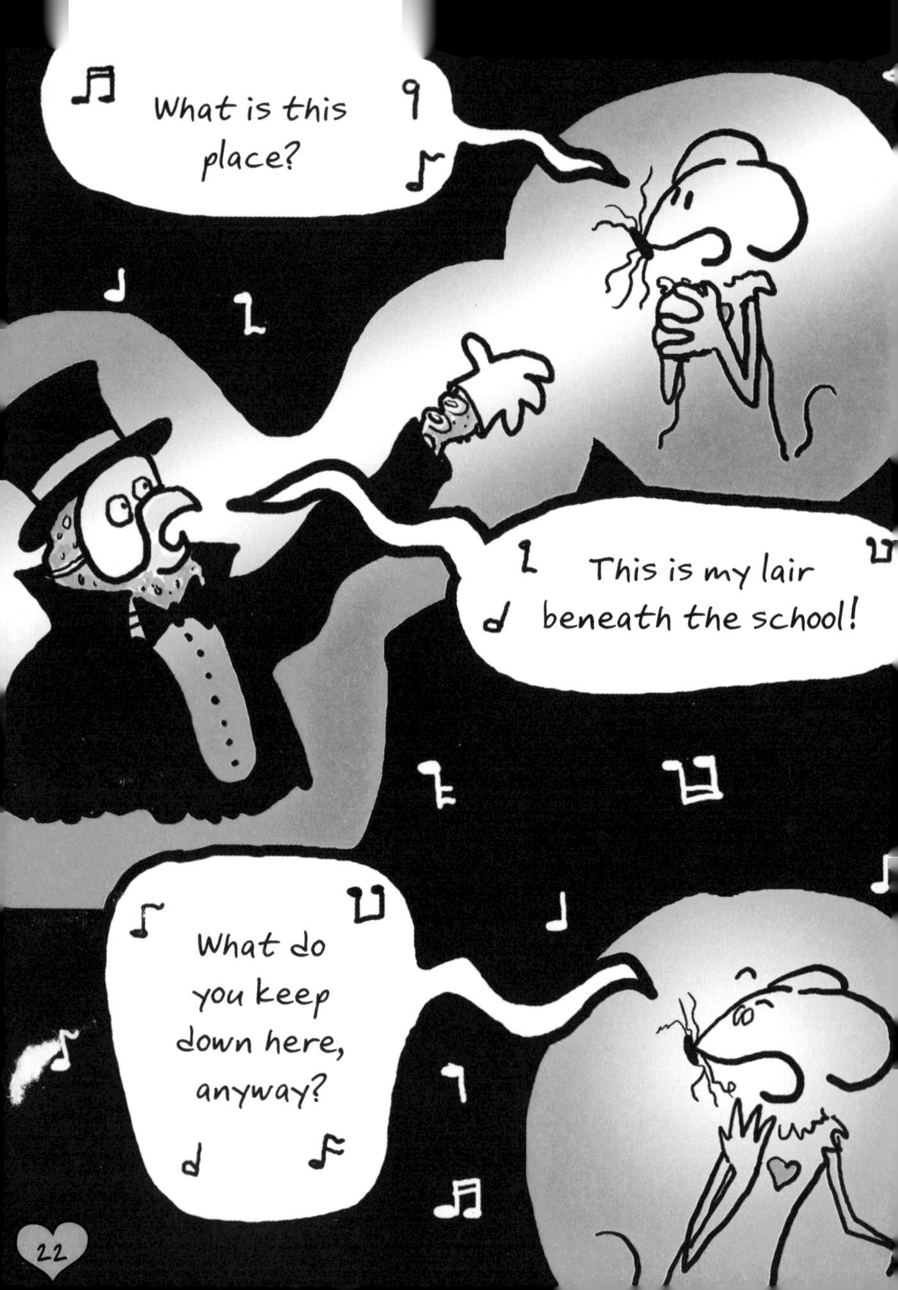
What is this place?
This is my lair beneath the school!
What do you keep down here, anyway?

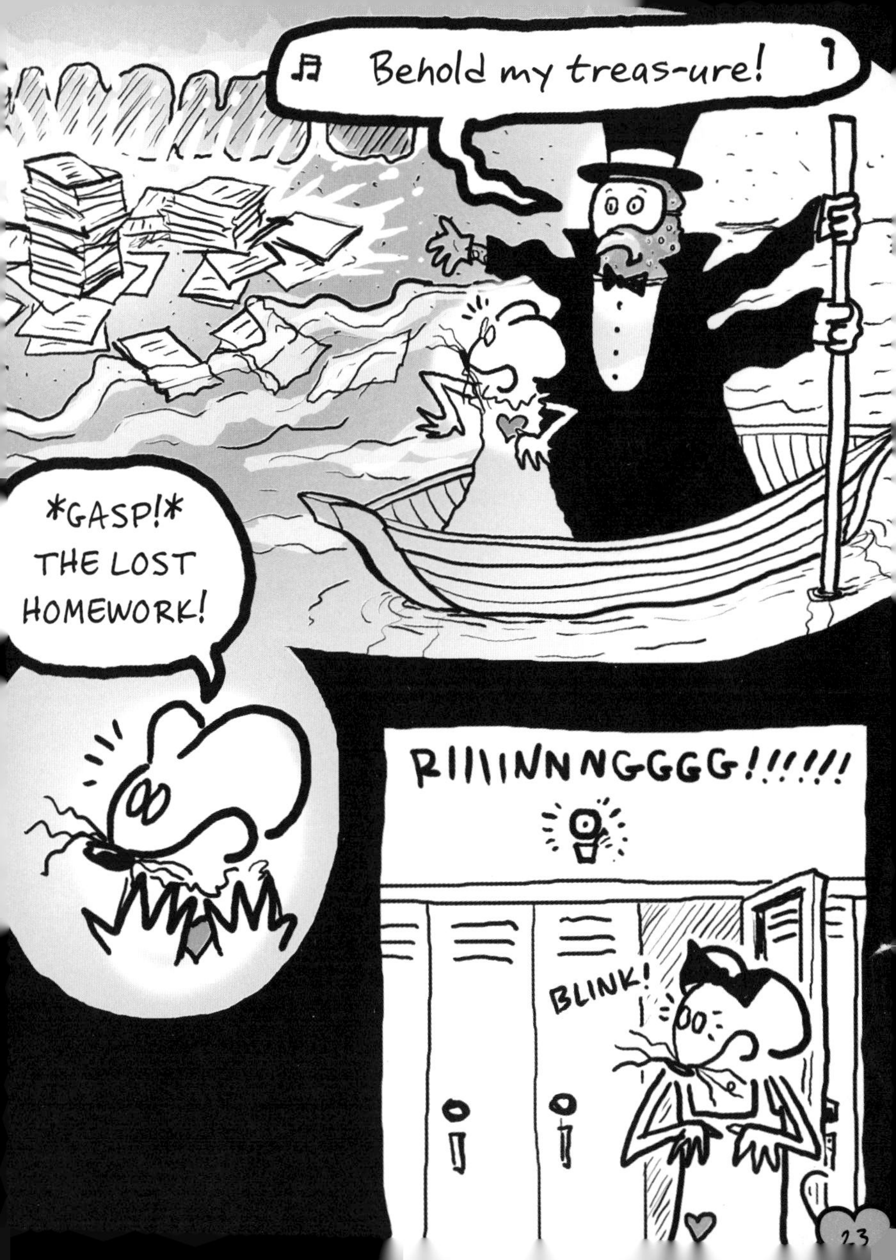

♫ Behold my treas-ure! ♪
*GASP!* THE LOST HOMEWORK!
RIIIINNNGGGG!!!!!!
BLINK!

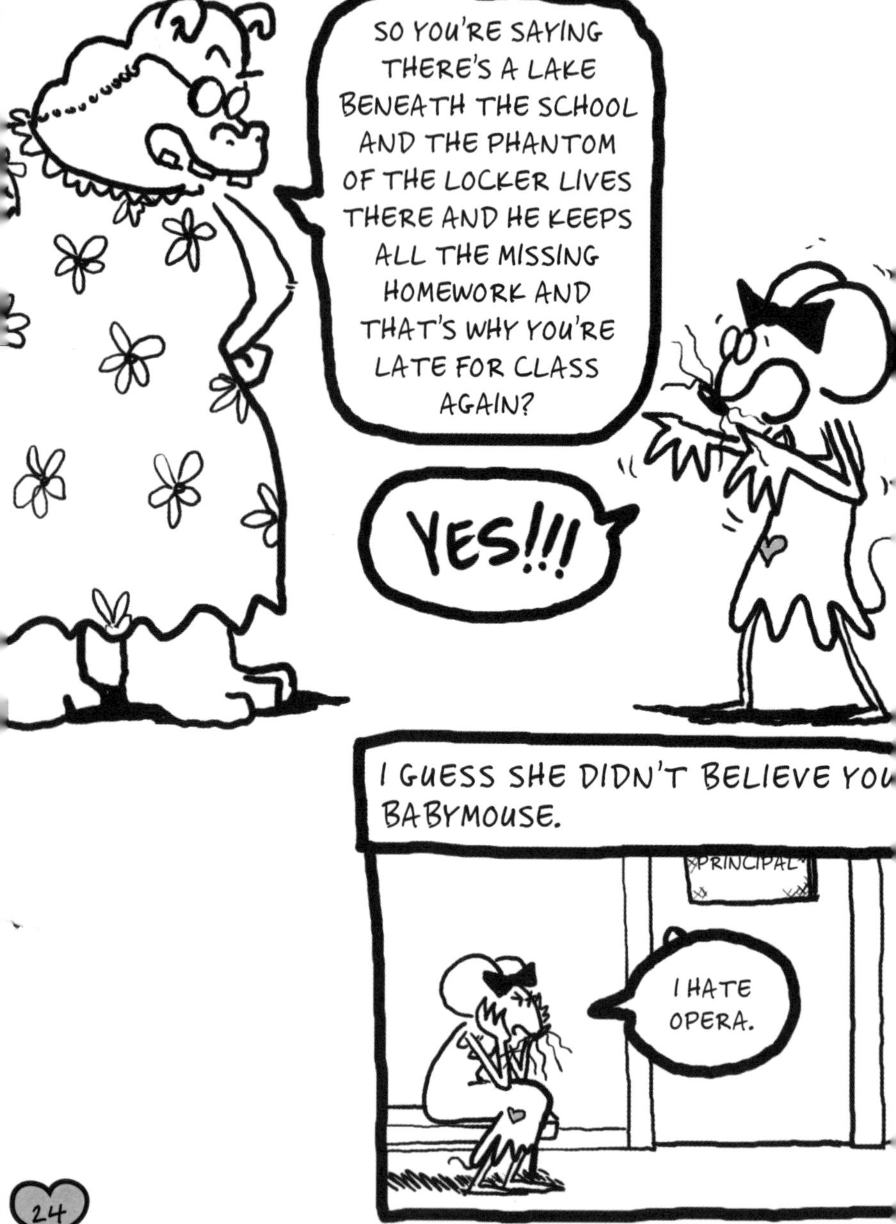
SO YOU'RE SAYING THERE'S A LAKE BENEATH THE SCHOOL AND THE PHANTOM OF THE LOCKER LIVES THERE AND HE KEEPS ALL THE MISSING HOMEWORK AND THAT'S WHY YOU'RE LATE FOR CLASS AGAIN?
YES!!!
I GUESS SHE DIDN'T BELIEVE YOU BABYMOUSE.
PRINCIPAL
I HATE OPERA.

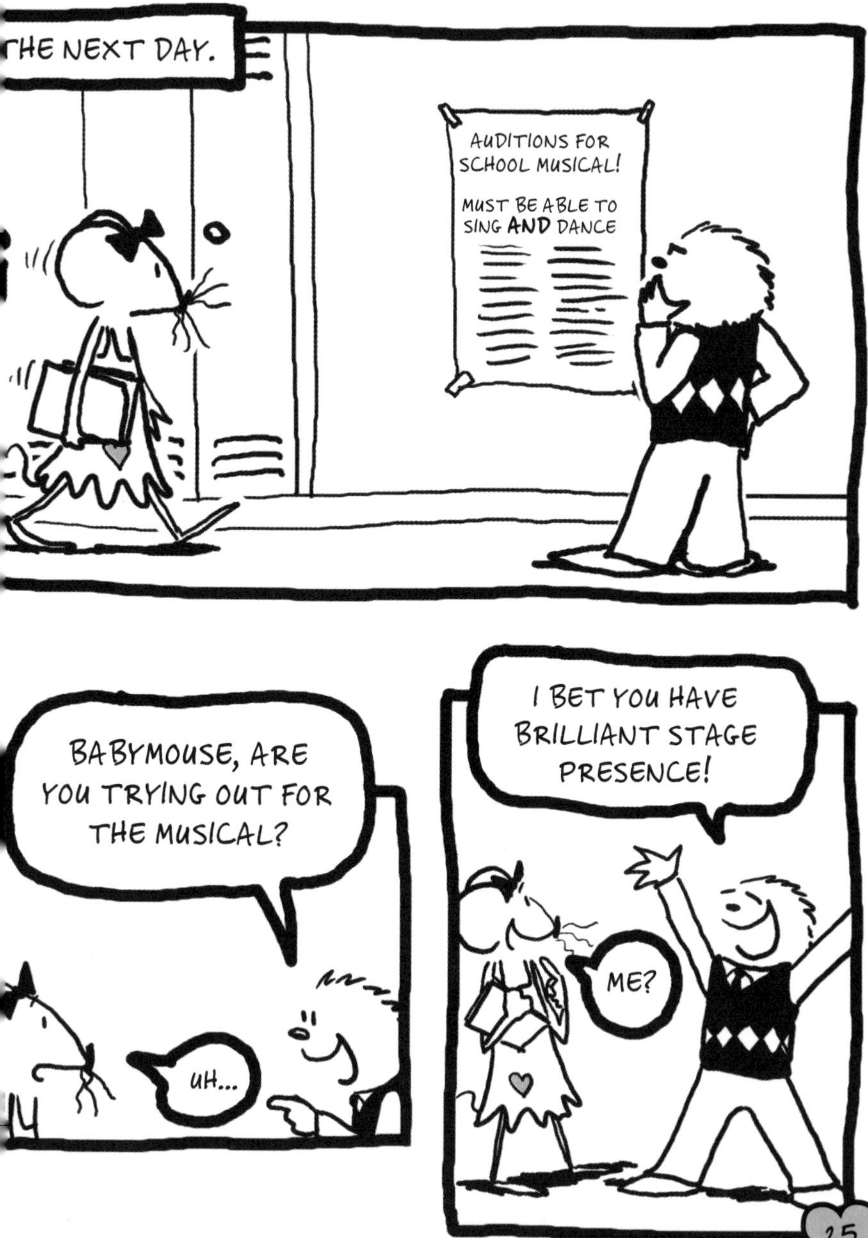
THE NEXT DAY.
AUDITIONS FOR SCHOOL MUSICAL!
MUST BE ABLE TO SING AND DANCE
BABYMOUSE, ARE YOU TRYING OUT FOR THE MUSICAL?
UH...
I BET YOU HAVE BRILLIANT STAGE PRESENCE!
ME?

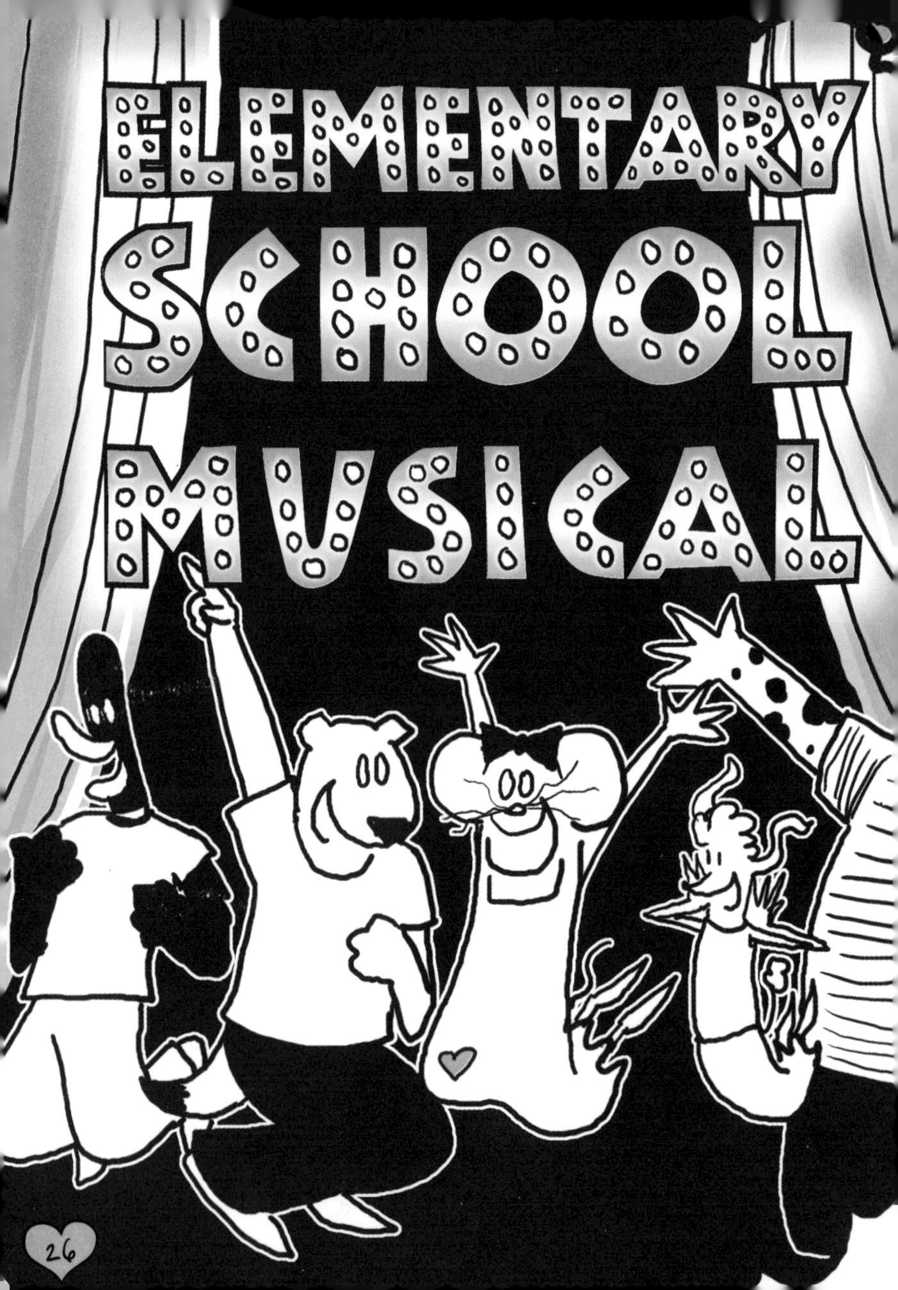
ELEMENTARY SCHOOL MUSICAL

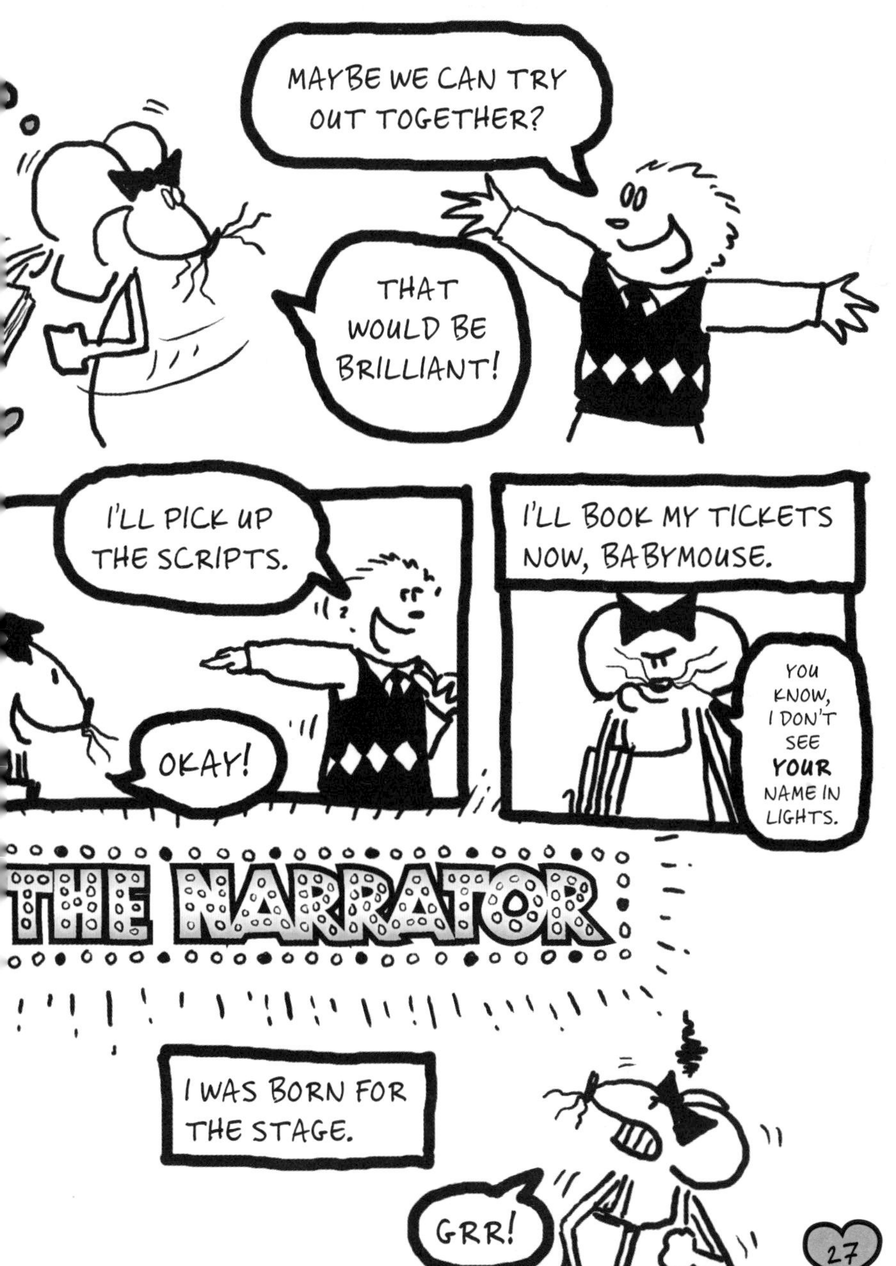
MAYBE WE CAN TRY OUT TOGETHER?
THAT WOULD BE BRILLIANT!
I'LL PICK UP THE SCRIPTS.
OKAY!
I'LL BOOK MY TICKETS NOW, BABYMOUSE.
YOU KNOW, I DON'T SEE **YOUR** NAME IN LIGHTS.
THE NARRATOR
I WAS BORN FOR THE STAGE.
GRR!

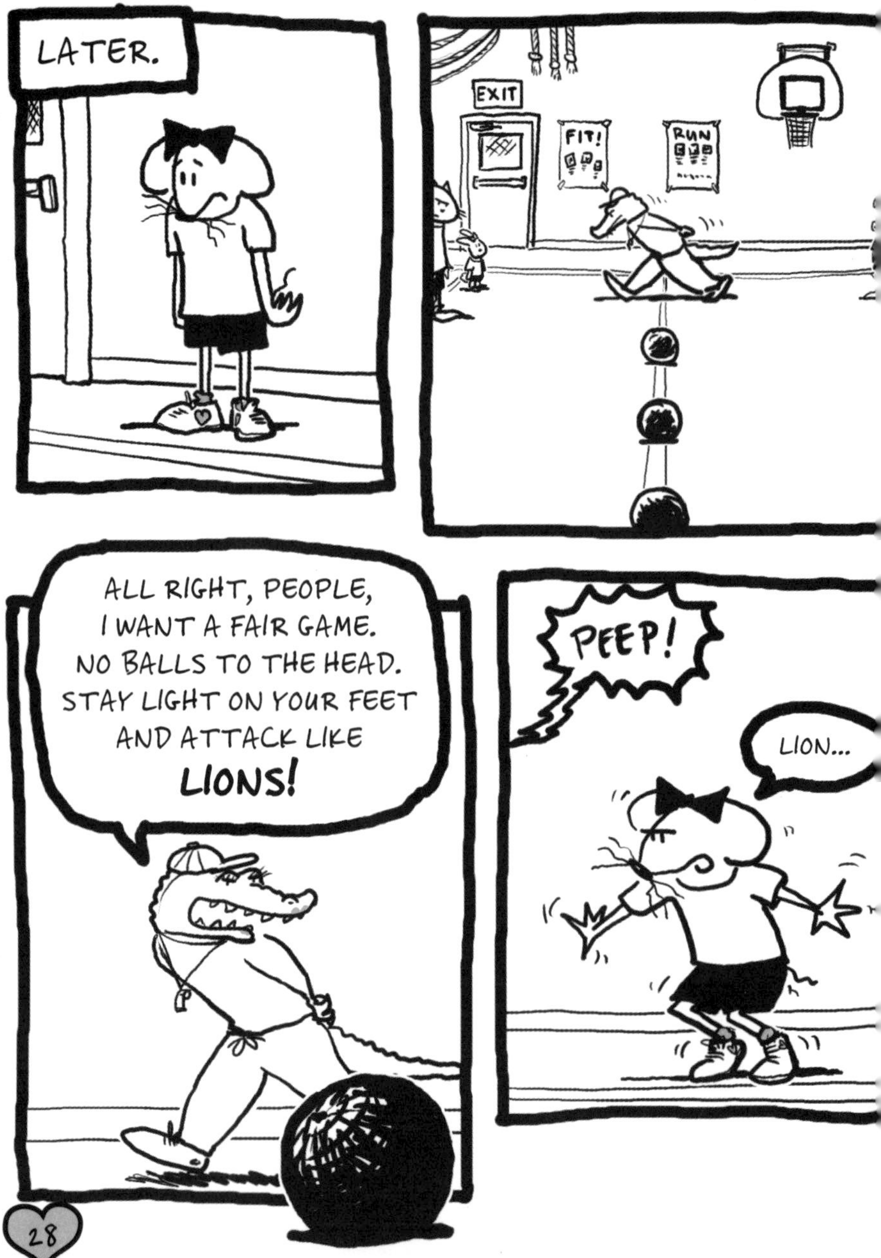
LATER.
EXIT
FIT!
RUN
ALL RIGHT, PEOPLE, I WANT A FAIR GAME. NO BALLS TO THE HEAD. STAY LIGHT ON YOUR FEET AND ATTACK LIKE **LIONS!**
PEEP!
LION...

TOM TOM TOM TOM TOM TOM
BRRRUUMMMMMMARU
TUM TOM TUM TA TOM
BRADA DADA
?

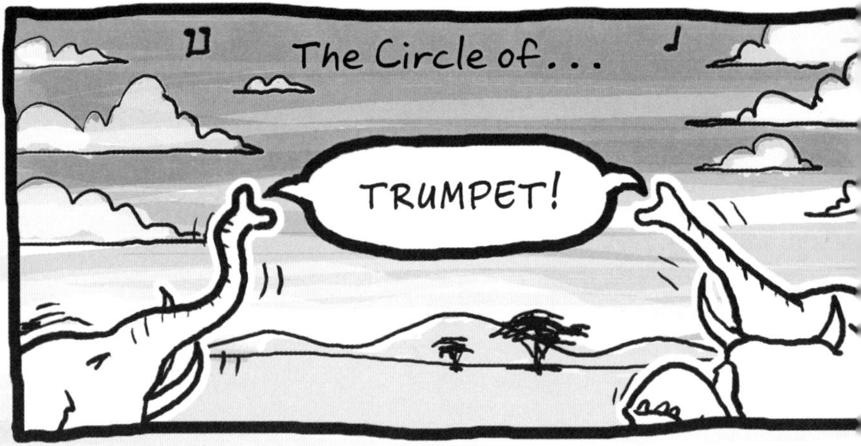
The Circle of...
TRUMPET!
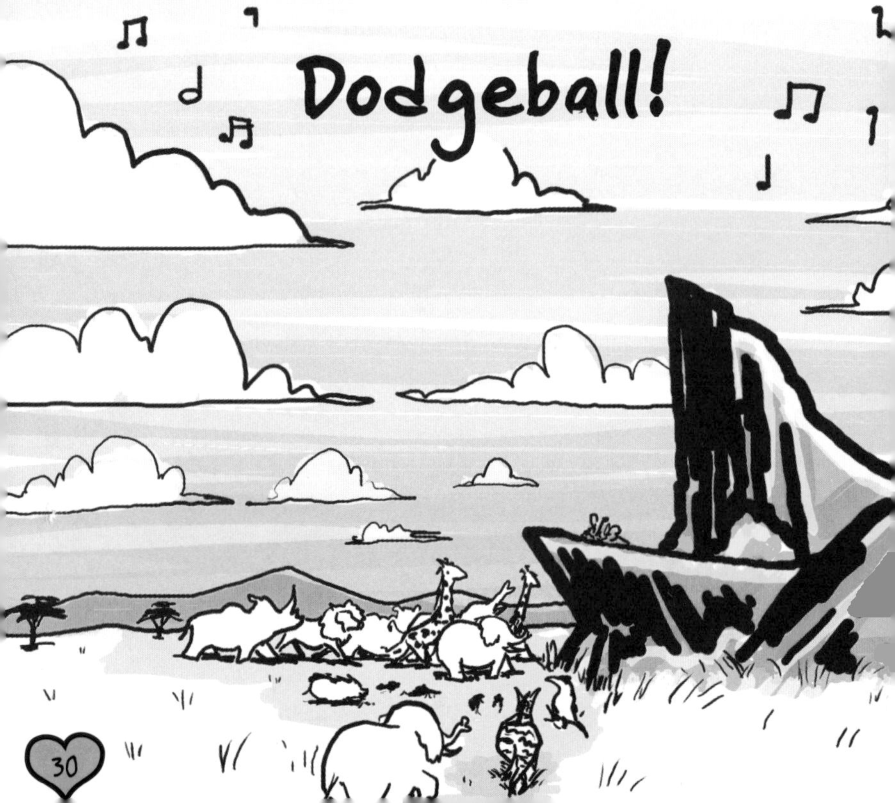
Dodgeball!

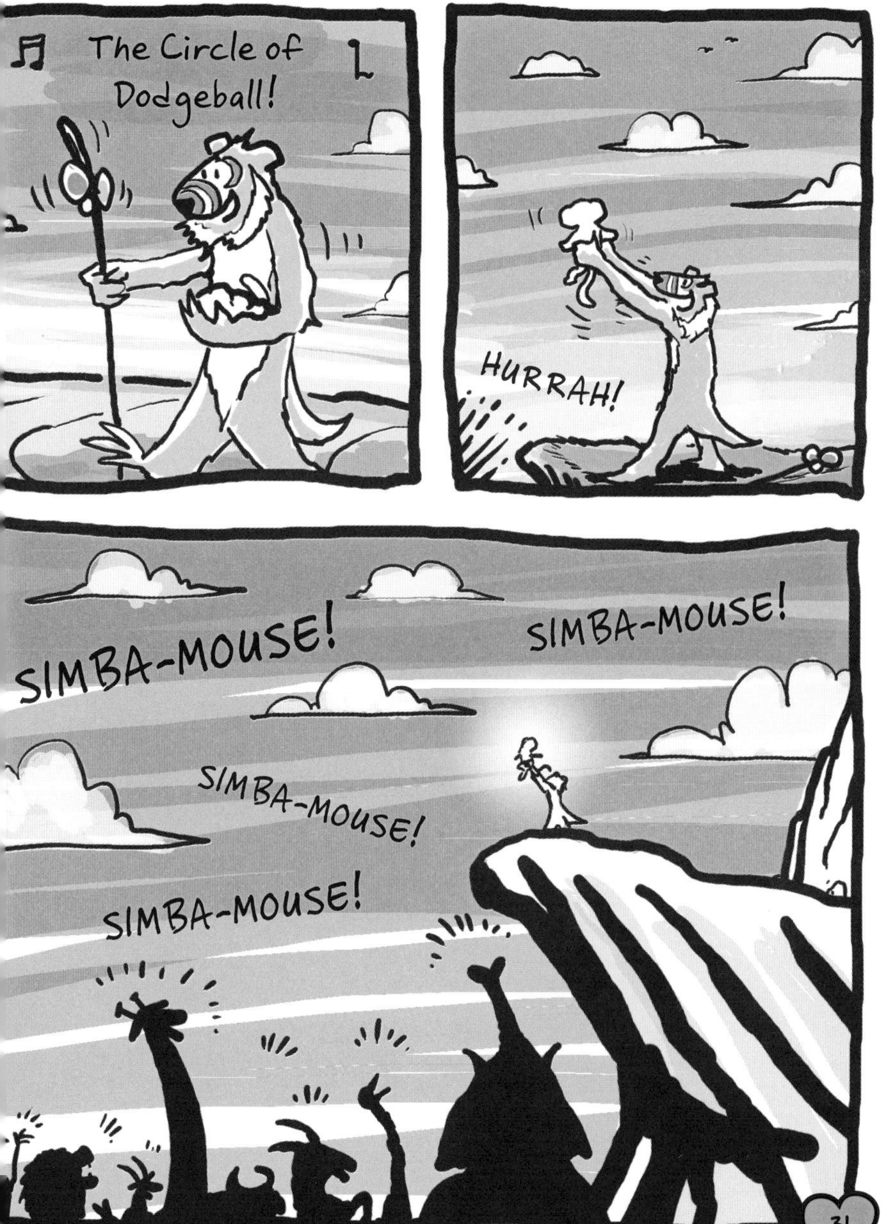
The Circle of Dodgeball!
HURRAH!
SIMBA-MOUSE!
SIMBA-MOUSE!
SIMBA-MOUSE!
SIMBA-MOUSE!

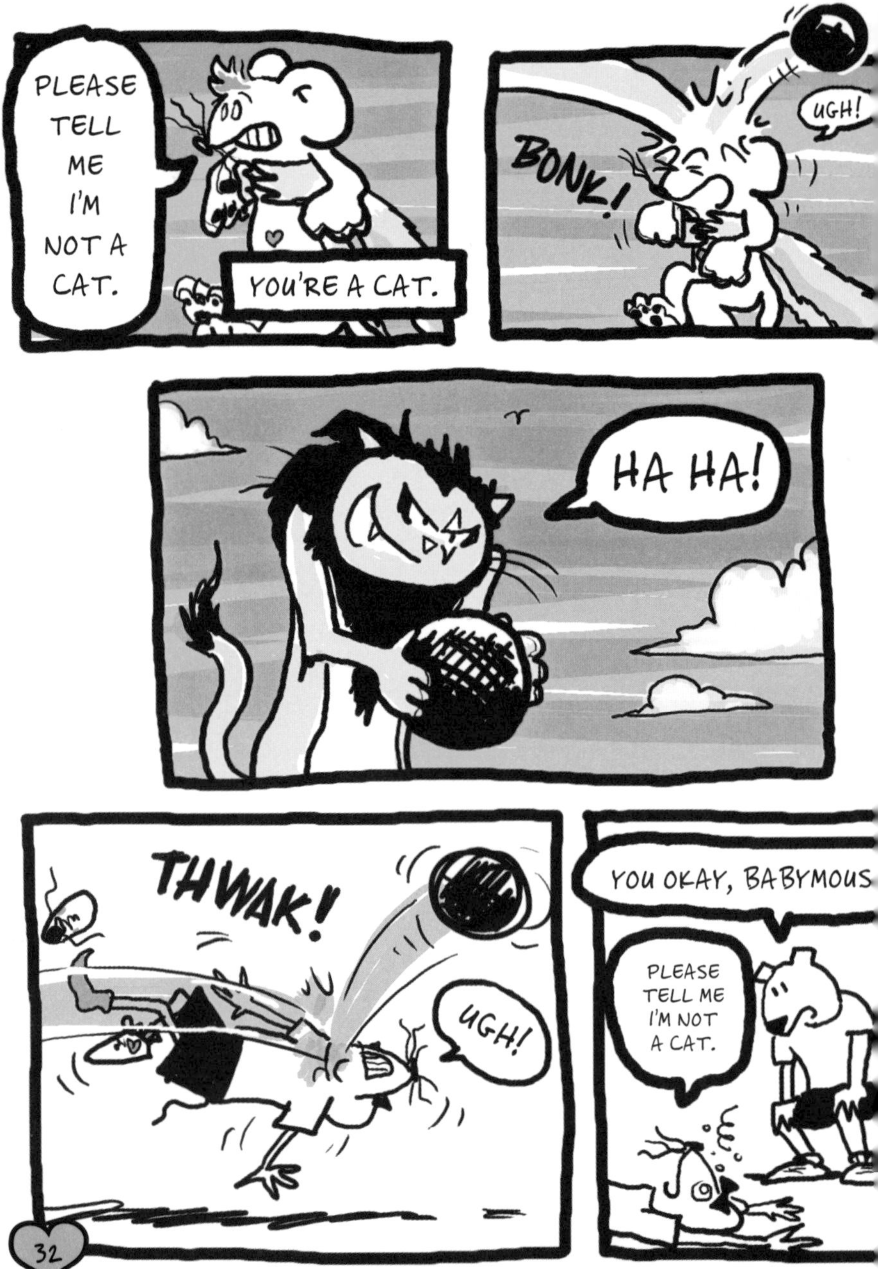
PLEASE TELL ME I'M NOT A CAT.
YOU'RE A CAT.
BONK!
UGH!
HA HA!
THWAK!
UGH!
YOU OKAY, BABYMOUS
PLEASE TELL ME I'M NOT A CAT.

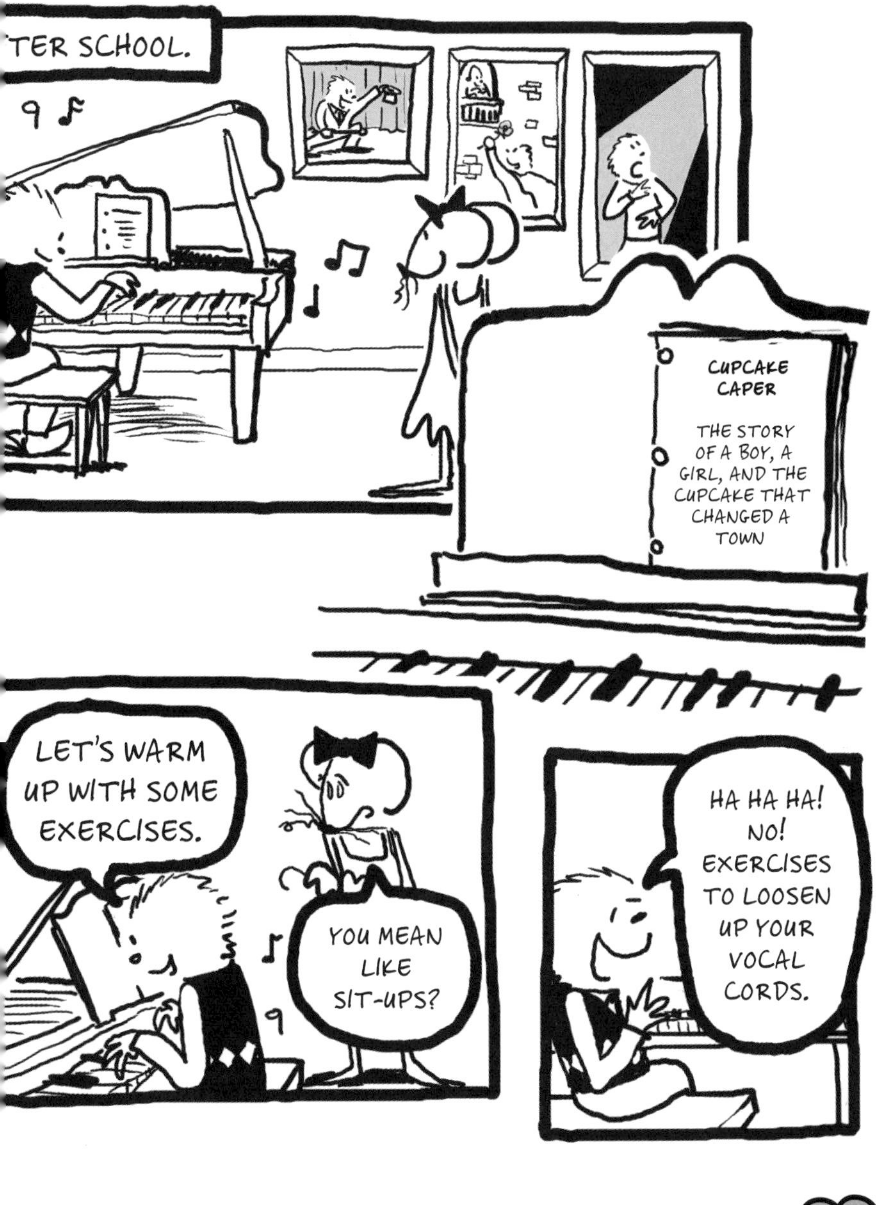

TER SCHOOL.
CUPCAKE CAPER
THE STORY OF A BOY, A GIRL, AND THE CUPCAKE THAT CHANGED A TOWN
LET'S WARM UP WITH SOME EXERCISES.
YOU MEAN LIKE SIT-UPS?
HA HA HA! NO! EXERCISES TO LOOSEN UP YOUR VOCAL CORDS.

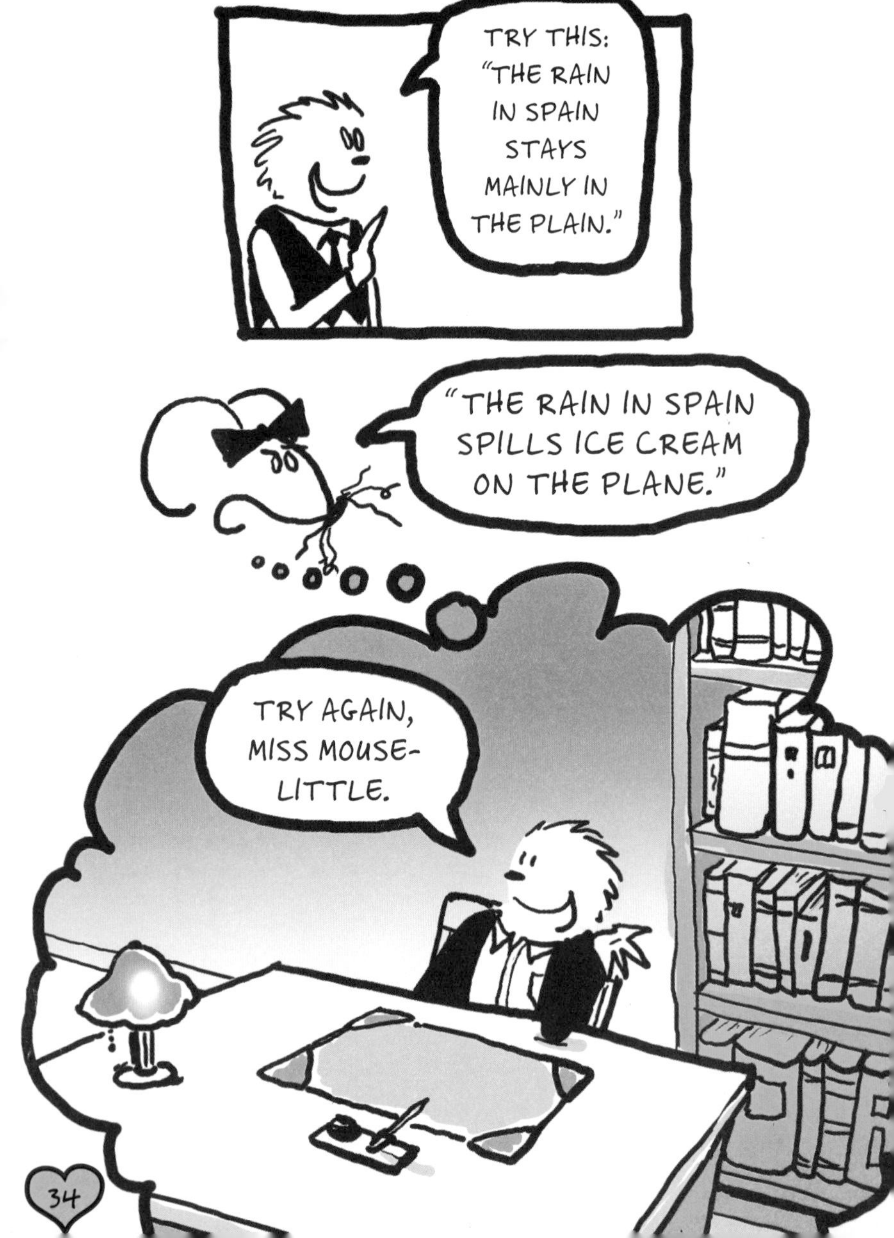
TRY THIS: "THE RAIN IN SPAIN STAYS MAINLY IN THE PLAIN."
"THE RAIN IN SPAIN SPILLS ICE CREAM ON THE PLANE."
TRY AGAIN, MISS MOUSE-LITTLE.

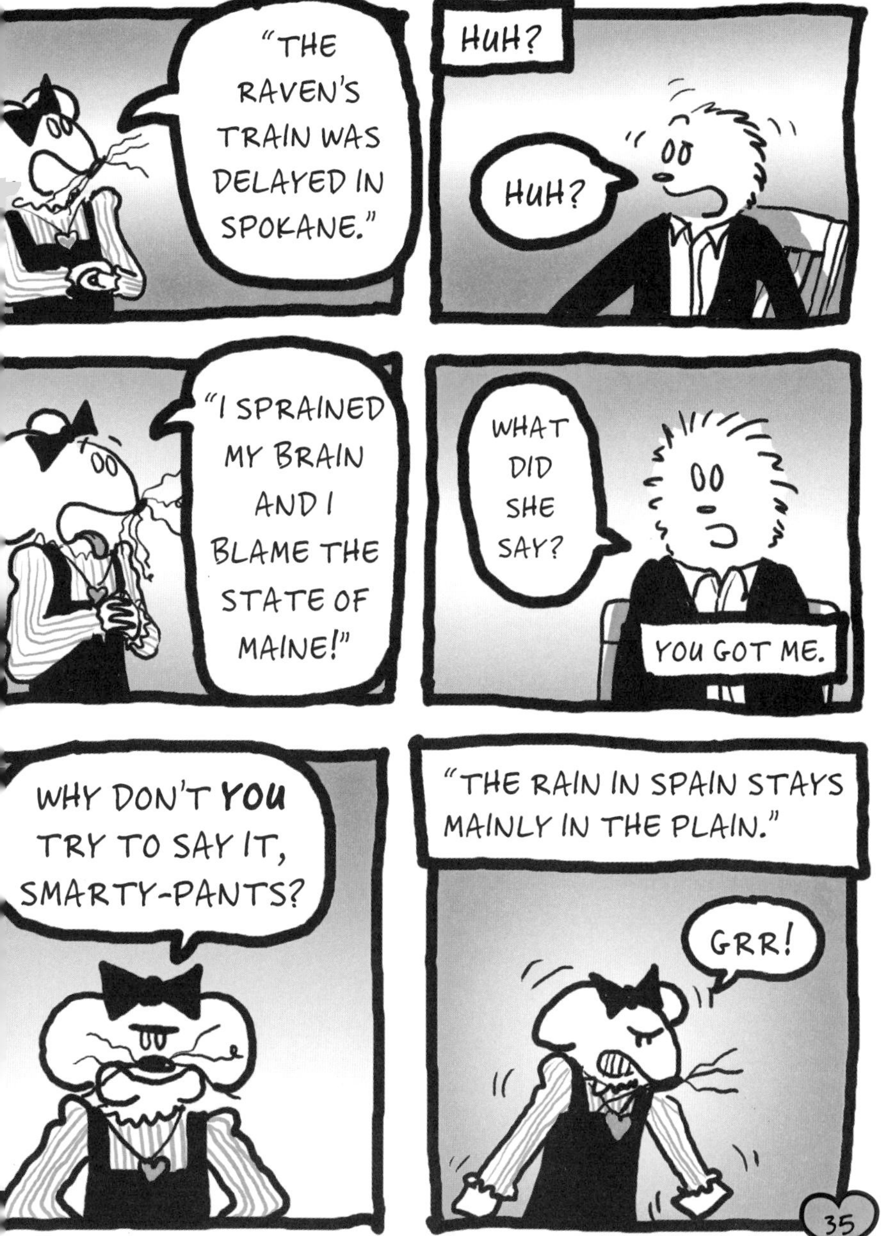
"THE RAVEN'S TRAIN WAS DELAYED IN SPOKANE."
HUH?
HUH?
"I SPRAINED MY BRAIN AND I BLAME THE STATE OF MAINE!"
WHAT DID SHE SAY?
YOU GOT ME.
WHY DON'T **YOU** TRY TO SAY IT, SMARTY-PANTS?
"THE RAIN IN SPAIN STAYS MAINLY IN THE PLAIN."
GRR!

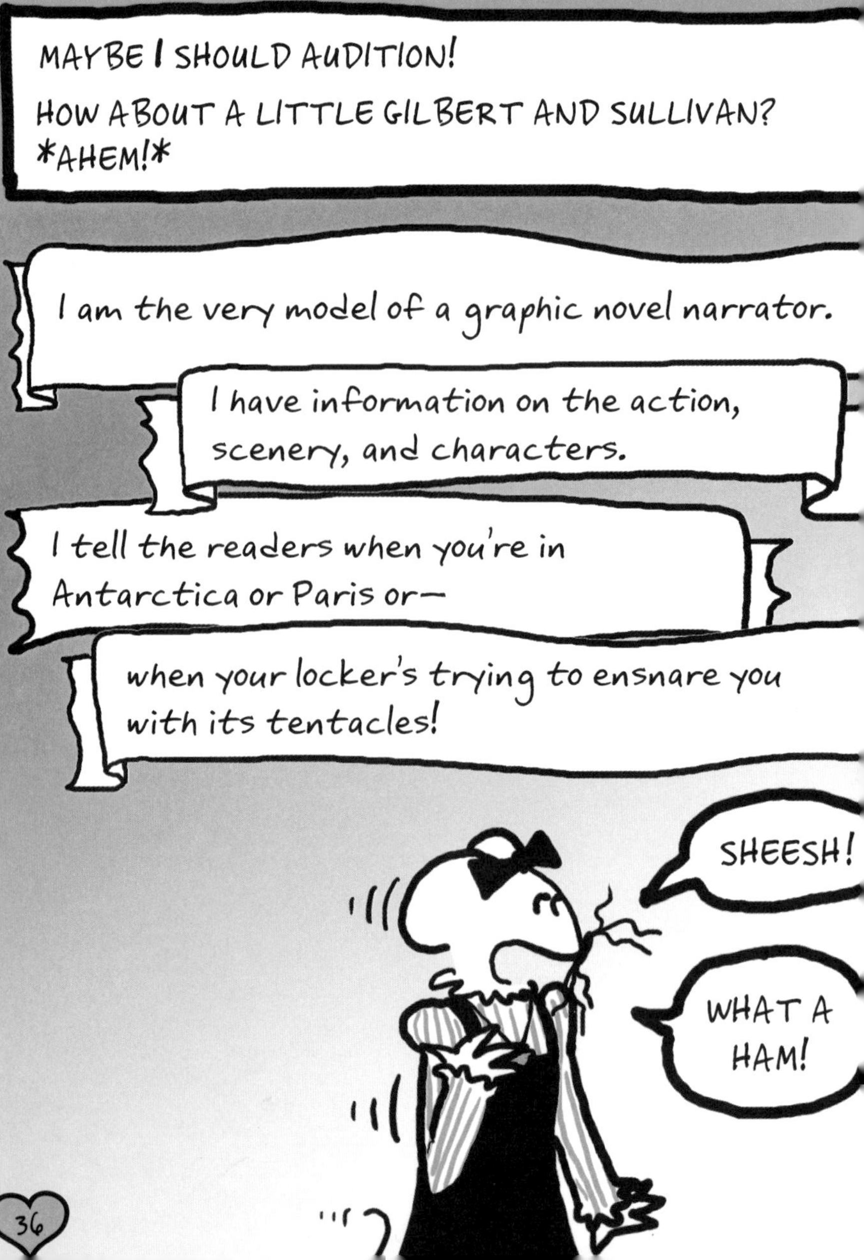
MAYBE I SHOULD AUDITION!
HOW ABOUT A LITTLE GILBERT AND SULLIVAN? *AHEM!*
I am the very model of a graphic novel narrator.
I have information on the action, scenery, and characters.
I tell the readers when you're in Antarctica or Paris or—
when your locker's trying to ensnare you with its tentacles!
SHEESH!
WHAT A HAM!

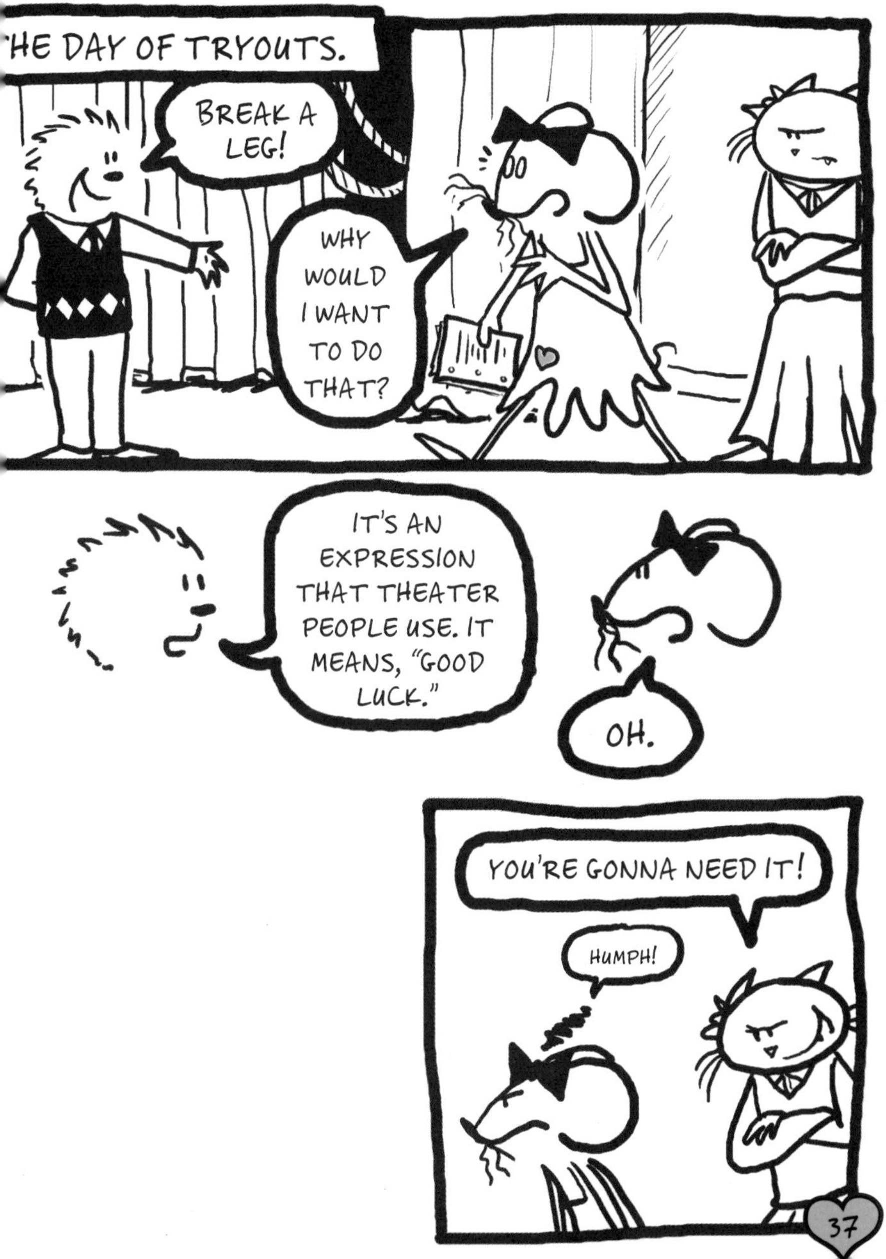

'HE DAY OF TRYOUTS.
BREAK A LEG!
WHY WOULD I WANT TO DO THAT?
IT'S AN EXPRESSION THAT THEATER PEOPLE USE. IT MEANS, "GOOD LUCK."
OH.
YOU'RE GONNA NEED IT!
HUMPH!

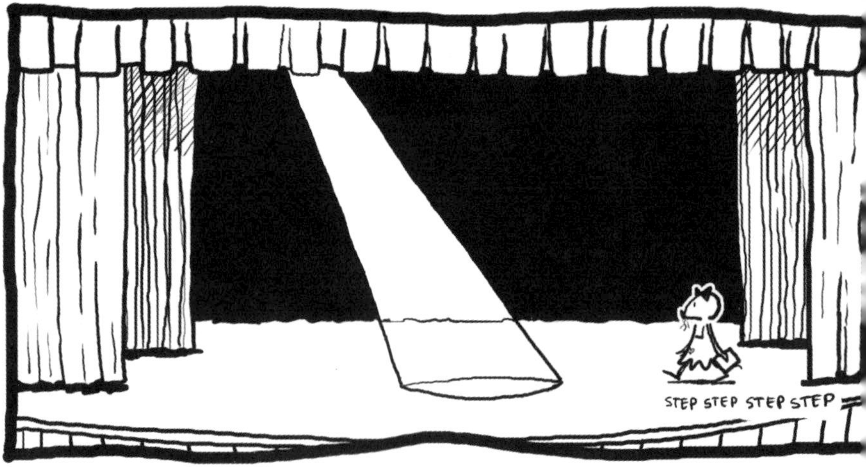
STEP STEP STEP STEP

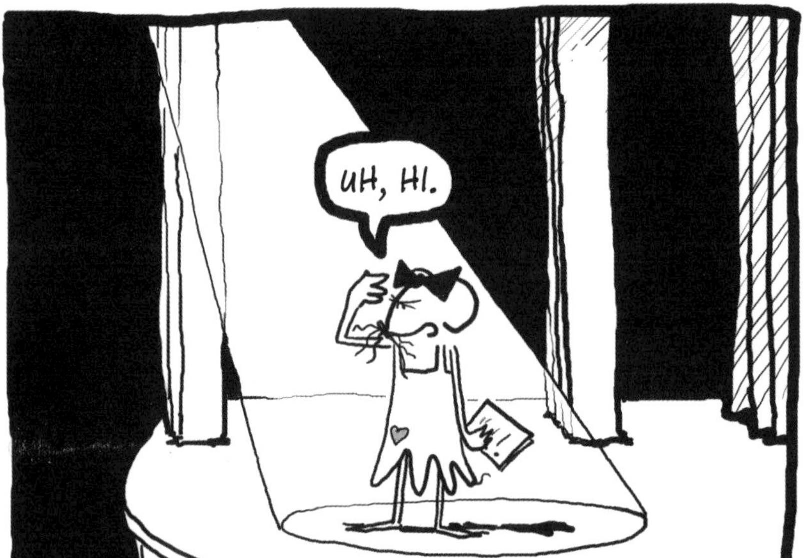
UH, HI.

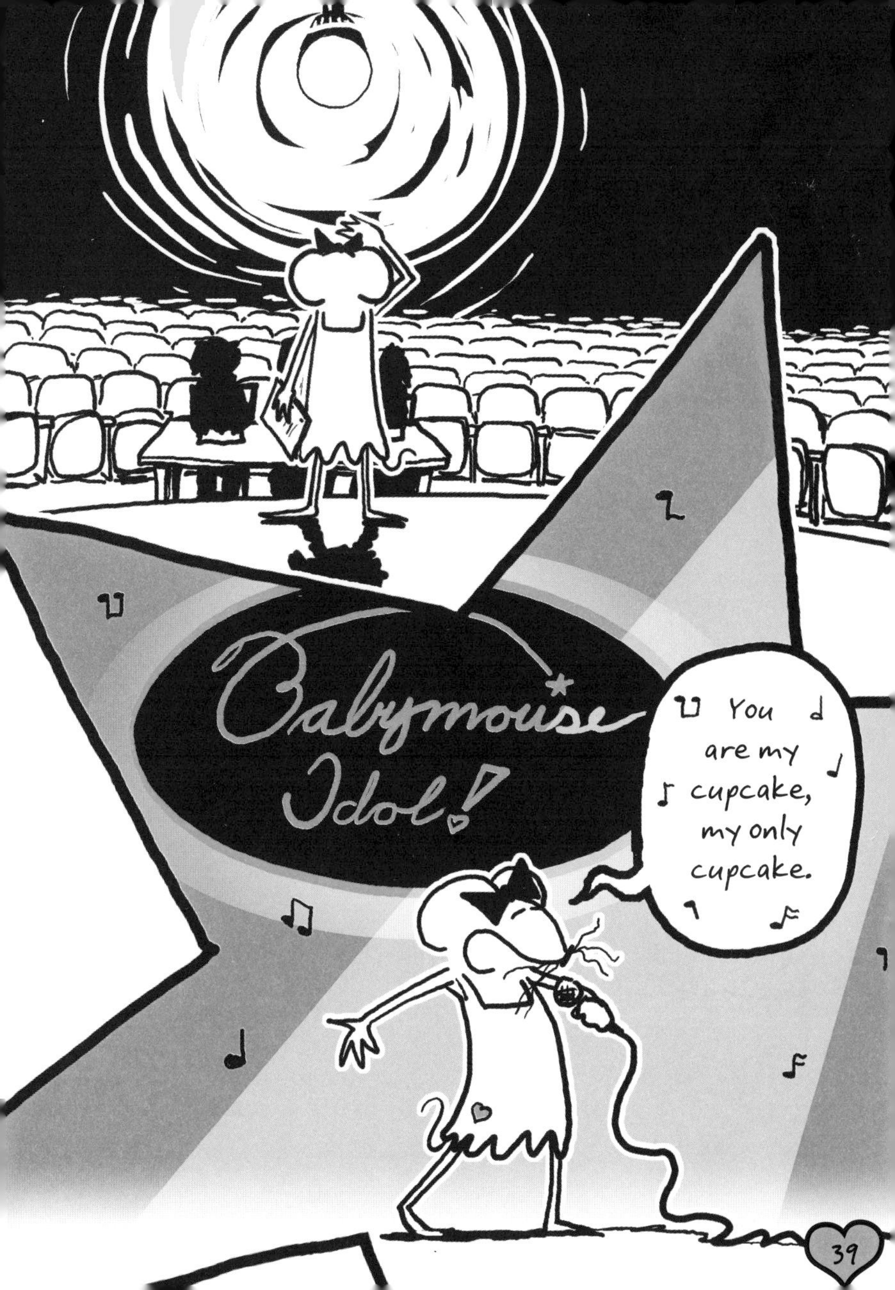
Babymouse Idol!
You are my cupcake, my only cupcake.

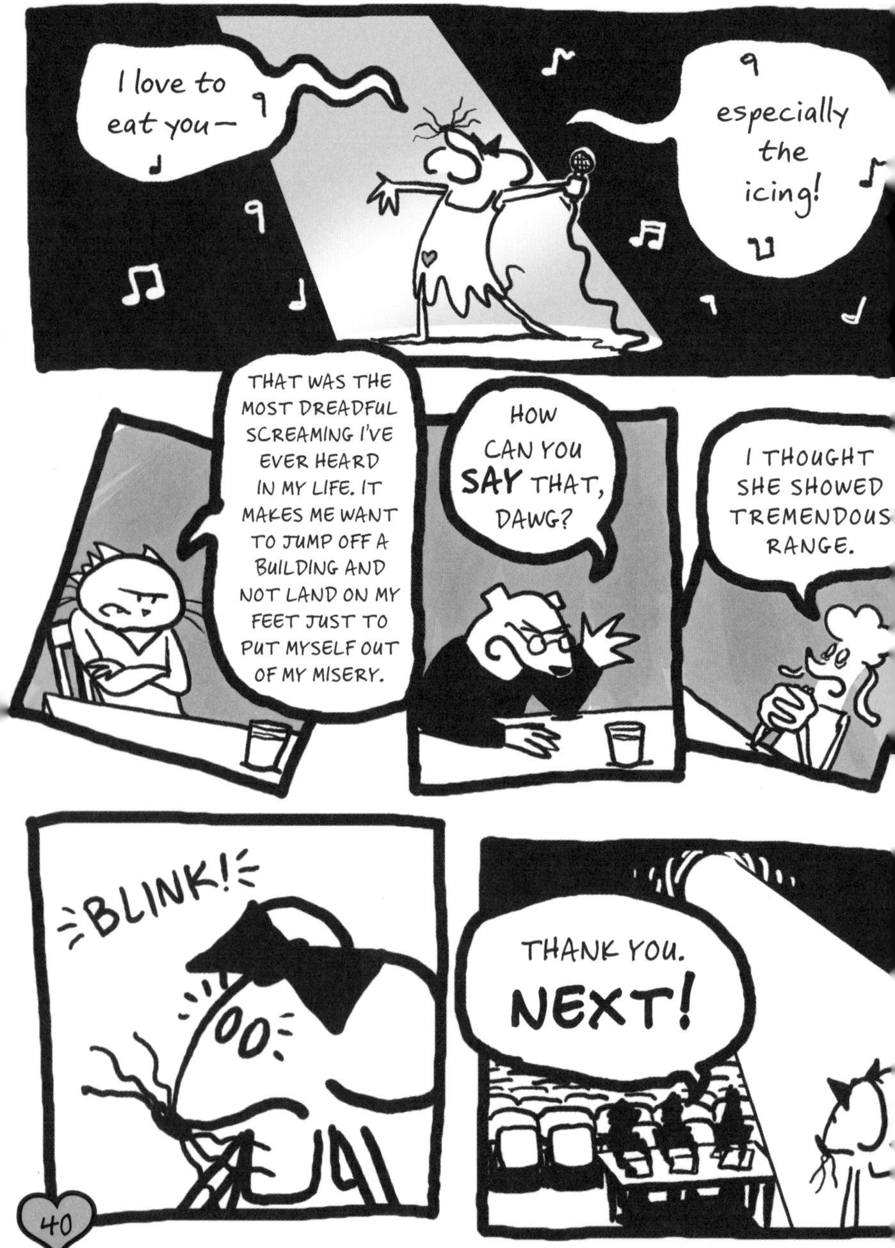

I love to eat you—
especially the icing!
THAT WAS THE MOST DREADFUL SCREAMING I'VE EVER HEARD IN MY LIFE. IT MAKES ME WANT TO JUMP OFF A BUILDING AND NOT LAND ON MY FEET JUST TO PUT MYSELF OUT OF MY MISERY.
HOW CAN YOU **SAY** THAT, DAWG?
I THOUGHT SHE SHOWED TREMENDOUS RANGE.
BLINK!
THANK YOU. **NEXT!**

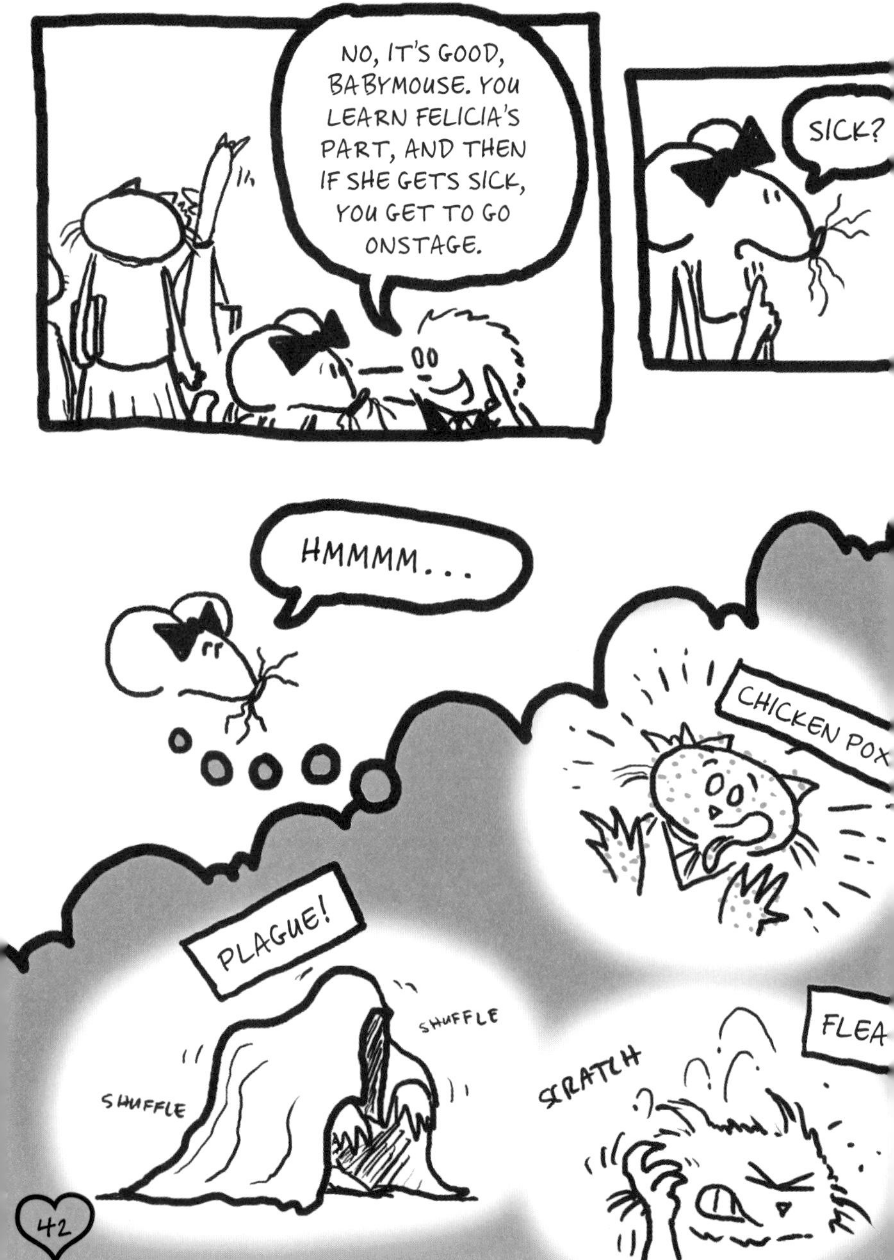
NO, IT'S GOOD, BABYMOUSE. YOU LEARN FELICIA'S PART, AND THEN IF SHE GETS SICK, YOU GET TO GO ONSTAGE.
SICK?
HMMMM...
CHICKEN POX
PLAGUE!
SHUFFLE
SHUFFLE
FLEA
SCRATCH

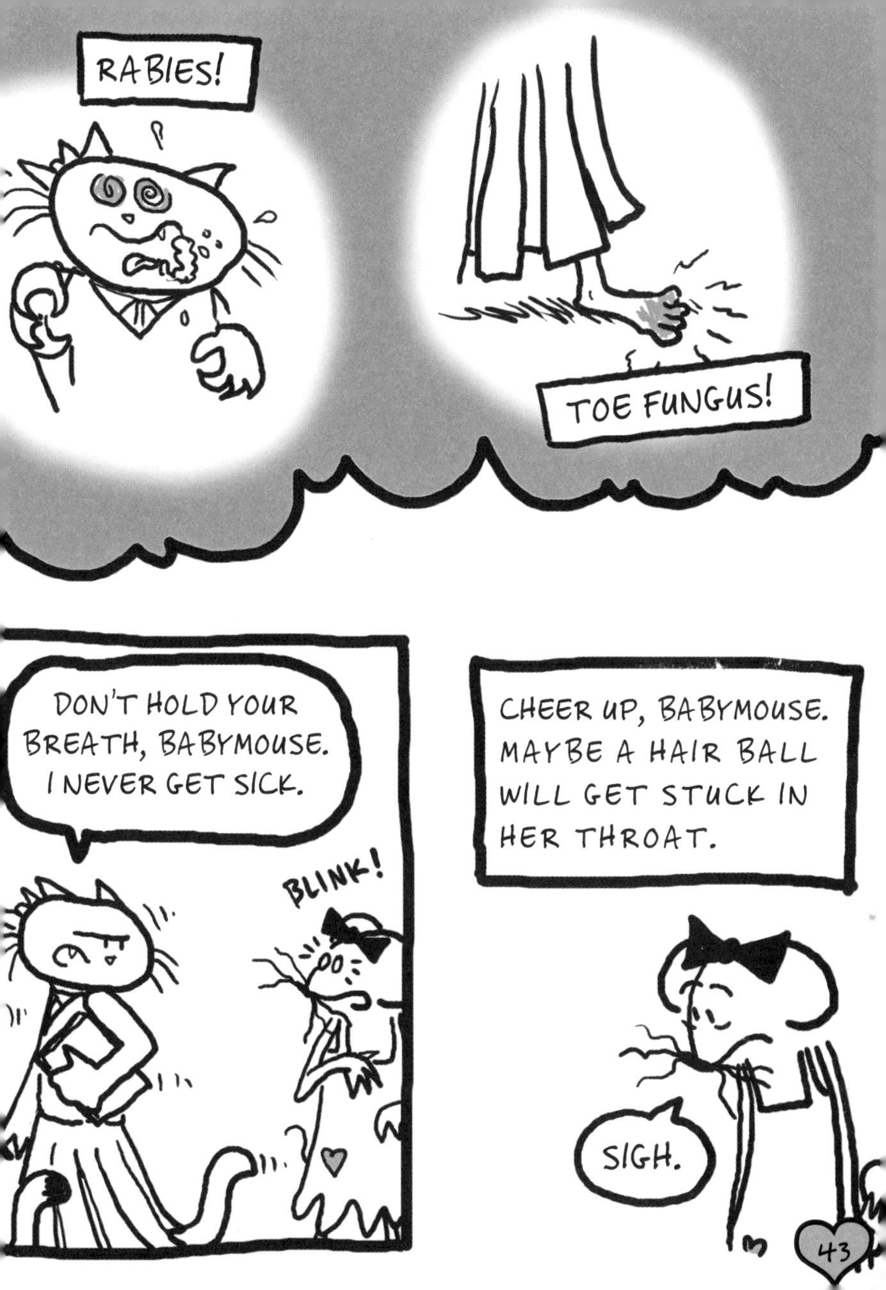
RABIES!
TOE FUNGUS!
DON'T HOLD YOUR BREATH, BABYMOUSE. I NEVER GET SICK.
BLINK!
CHEER UP, BABYMOUSE. MAYBE A HAIR BALL WILL GET STUCK IN HER THROAT.
SIGH.

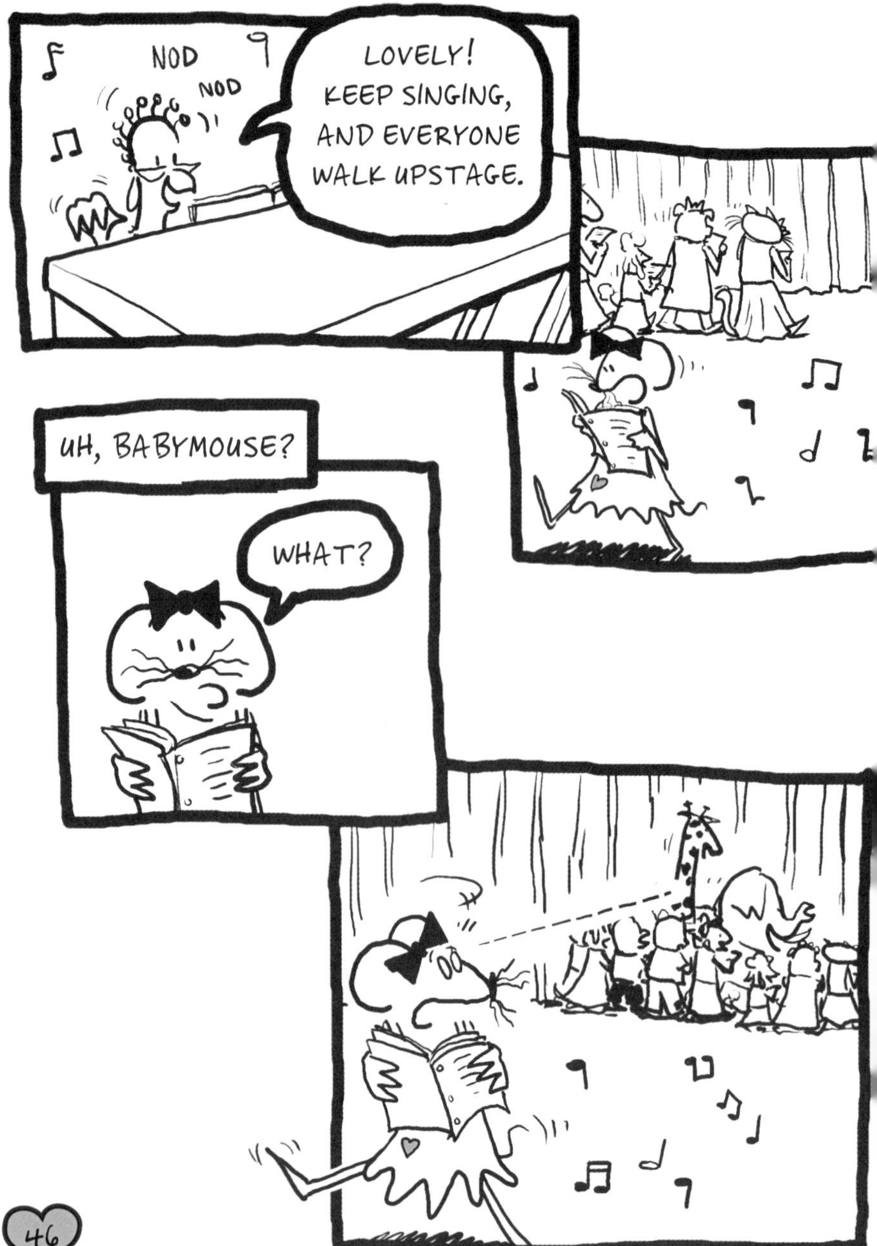
NOD
NOD
LOVELY! KEEP SINGING, AND EVERYONE WALK UPSTAGE.
UH, BABYMOUSE?
WHAT?

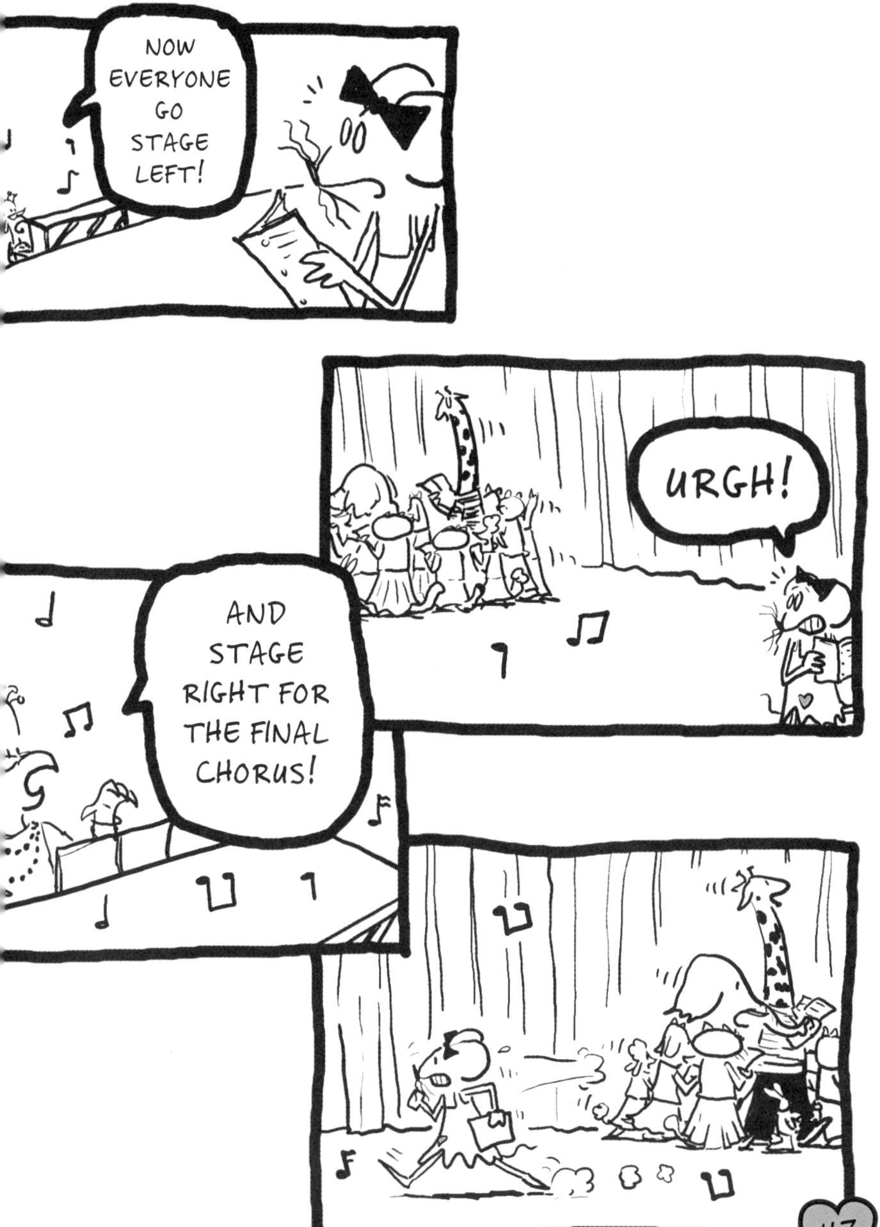
NOW EVERYONE GO STAGE LEFT!
URGH!
AND STAGE RIGHT FOR THE FINAL CHORUS!

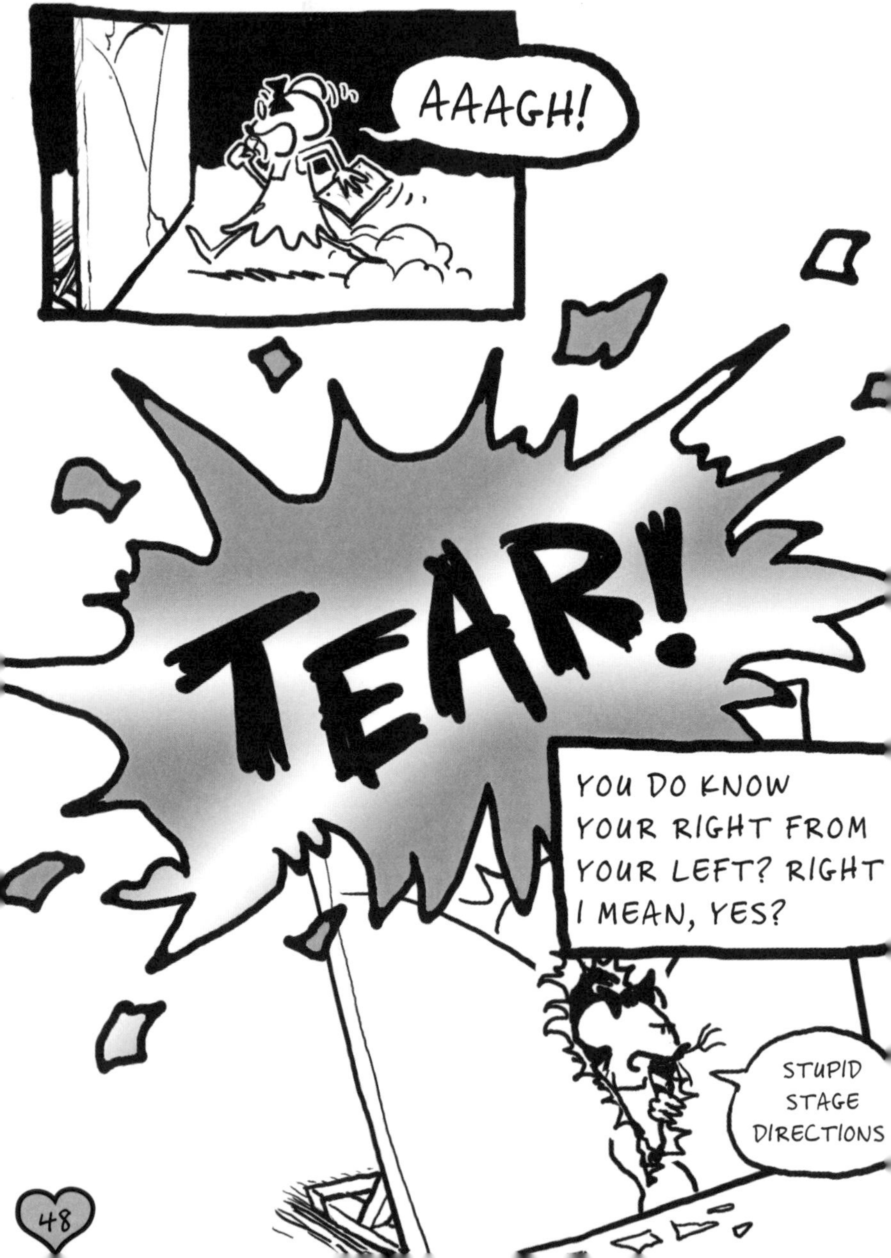
AAAGH!
TEAR!
YOU DO KNOW YOUR RIGHT FROM YOUR LEFT? RIGHT I MEAN, YES?
STUPID STAGE DIRECTIONS

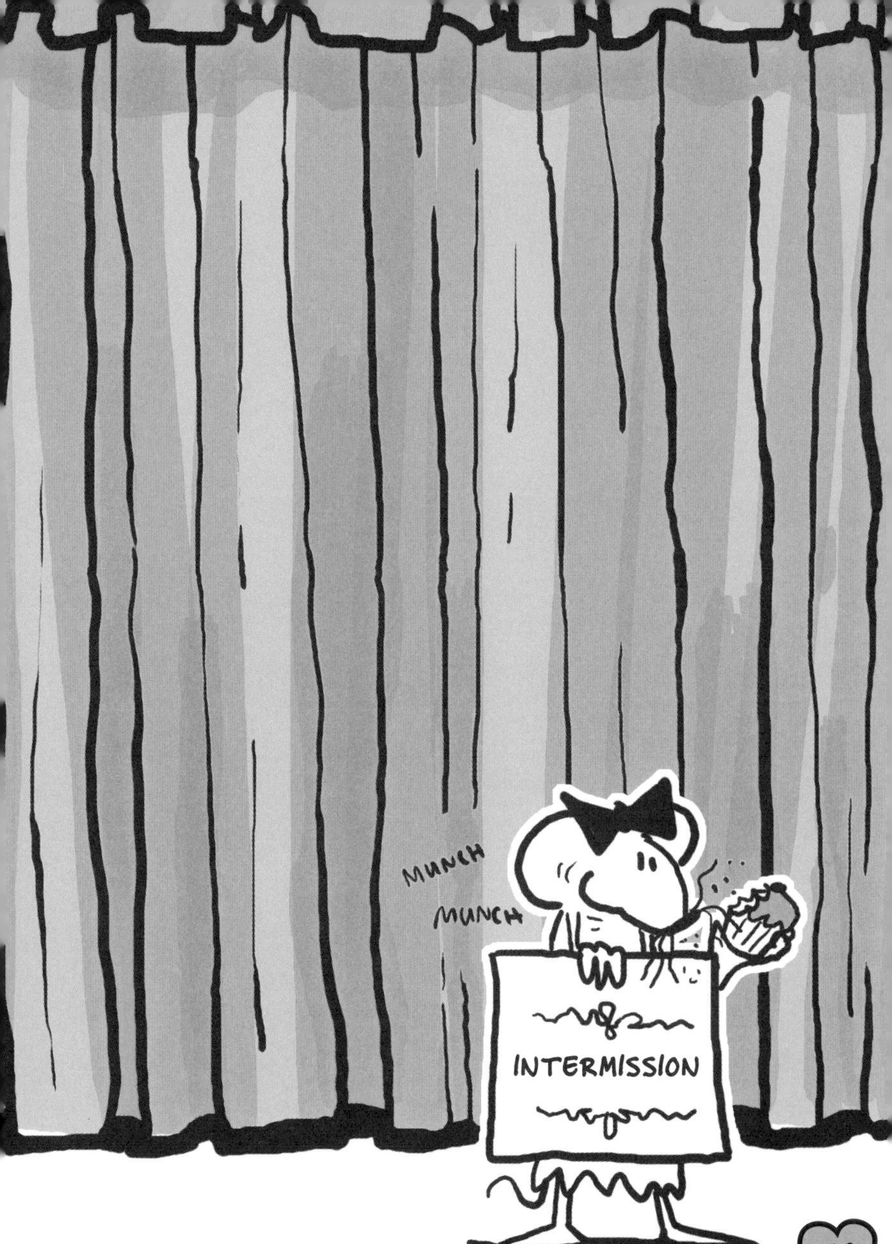
MUNCH
MUNCH
INTERMISSION

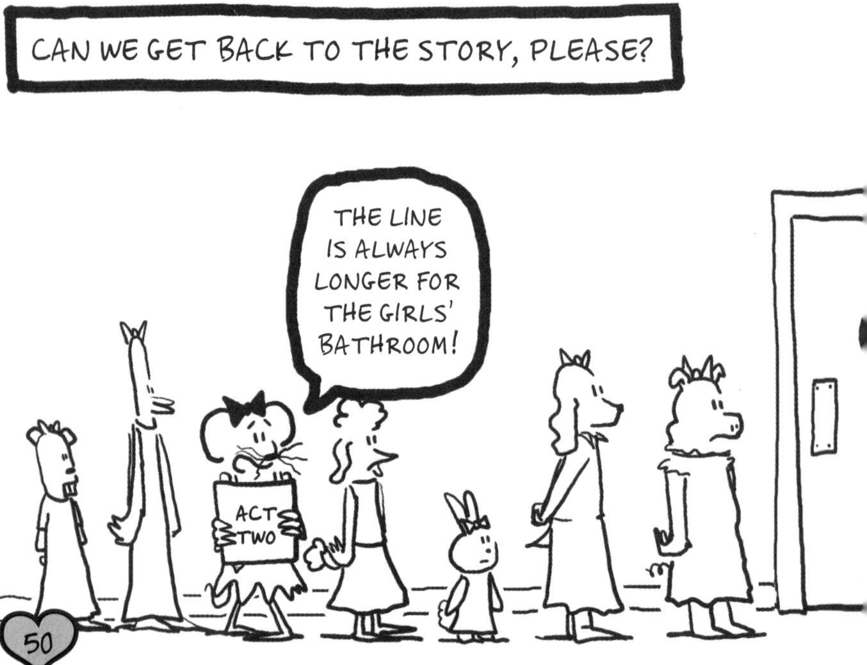
CAN WE GET BACK TO THE STORY, PLEASE?
THE LINE IS ALWAYS LONGER FOR THE GIRLS' BATHROOM!
ACT TWO

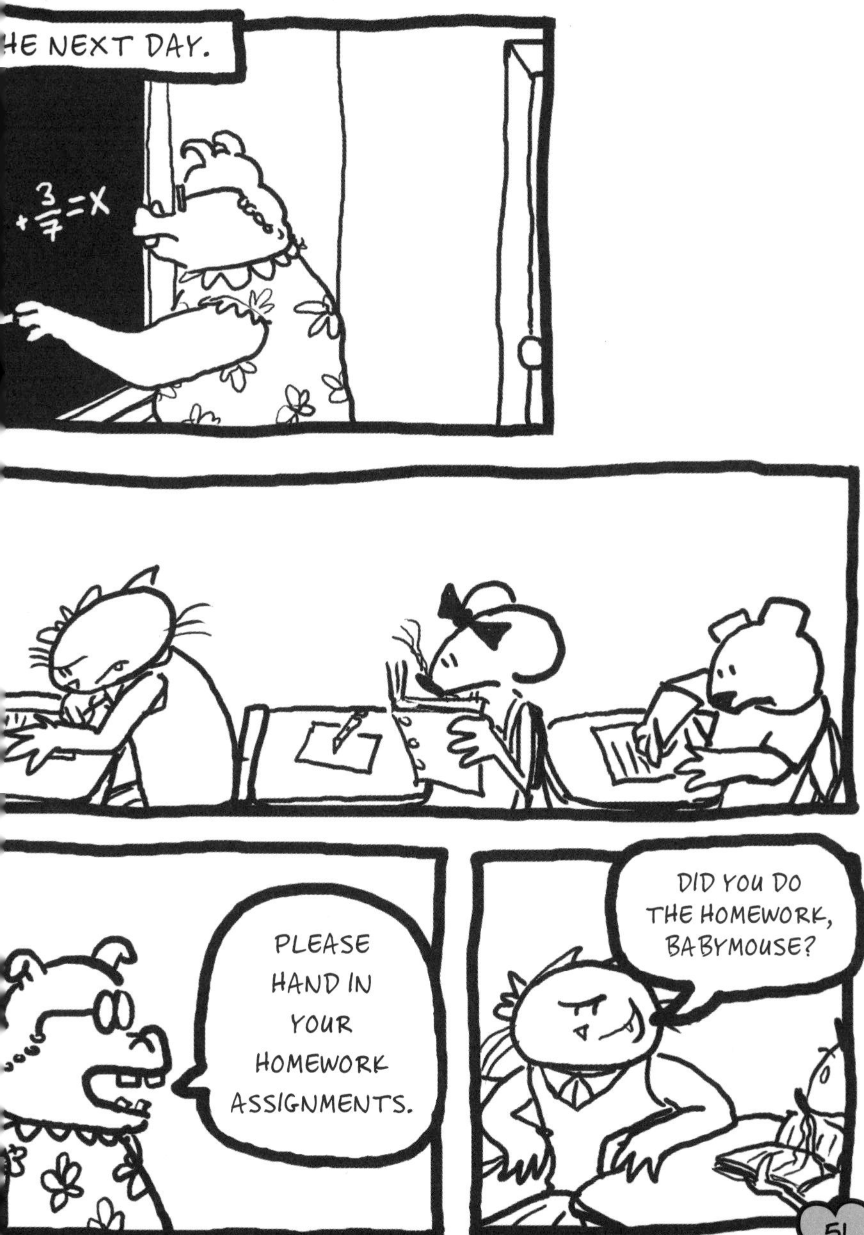

HE NEXT DAY.
$\frac{3}{7} = X$
PLEASE HAND IN YOUR HOMEWORK ASSIGNMENTS.
DID YOU DO THE HOMEWORK, BABYMOUSE?

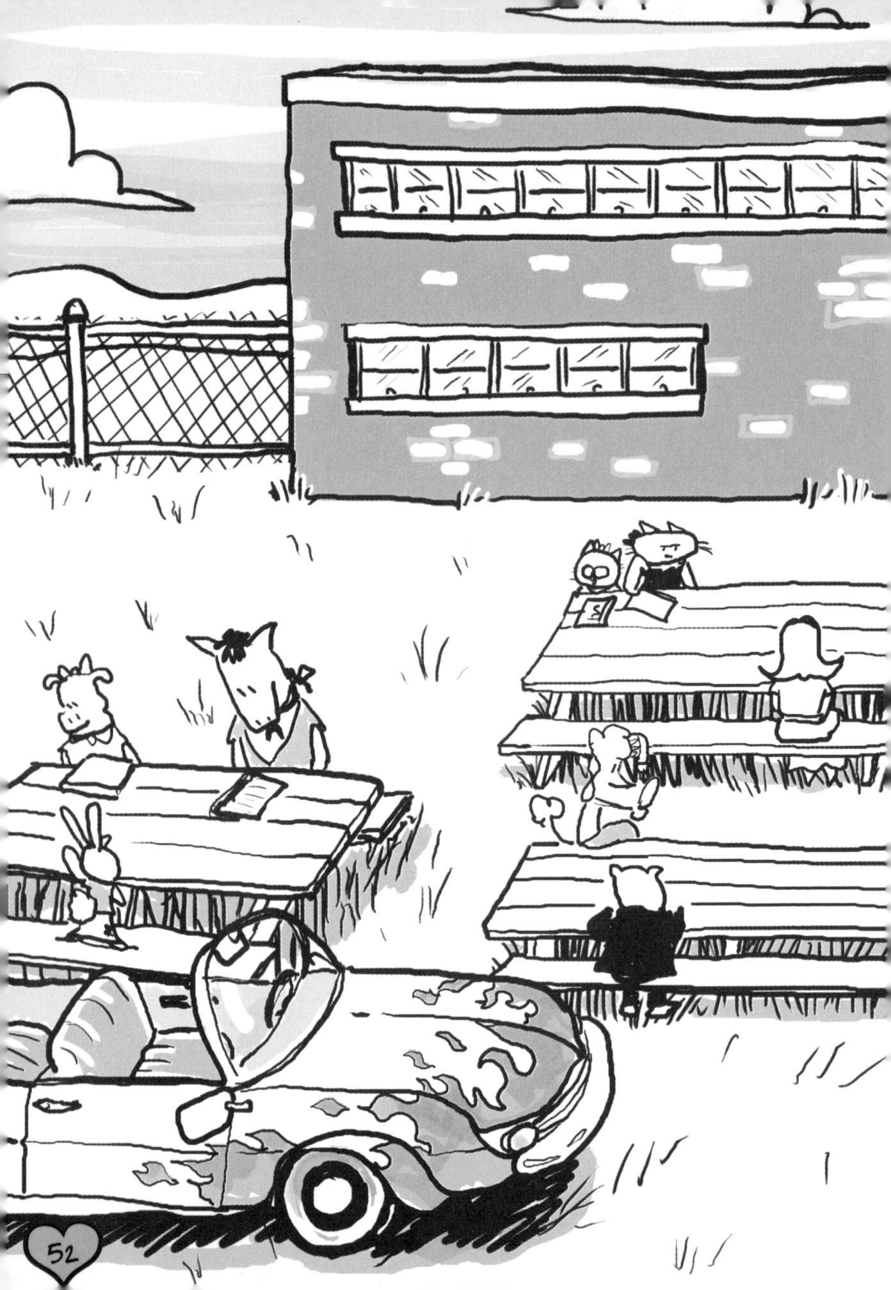

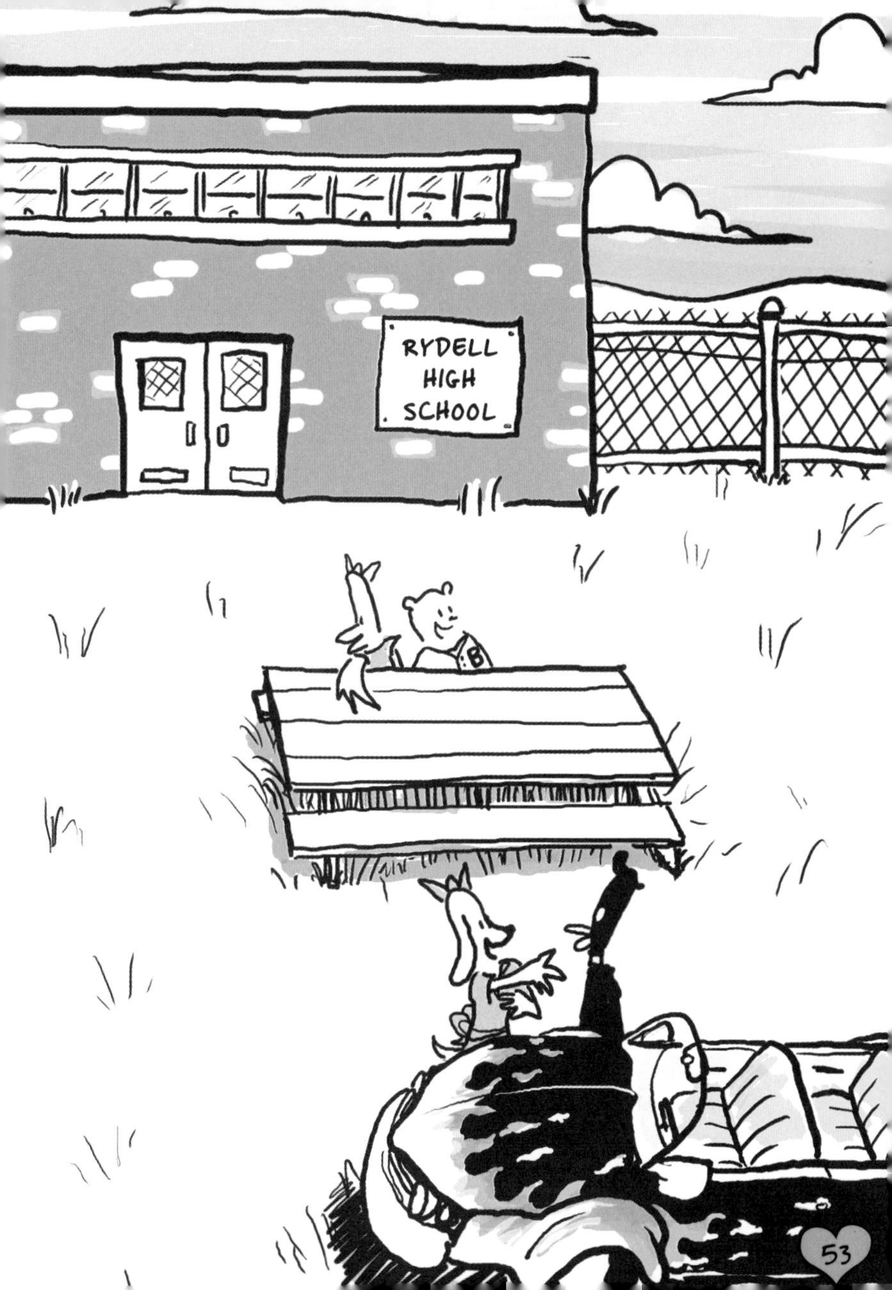
RYDELL
HIGH
SCHOOL

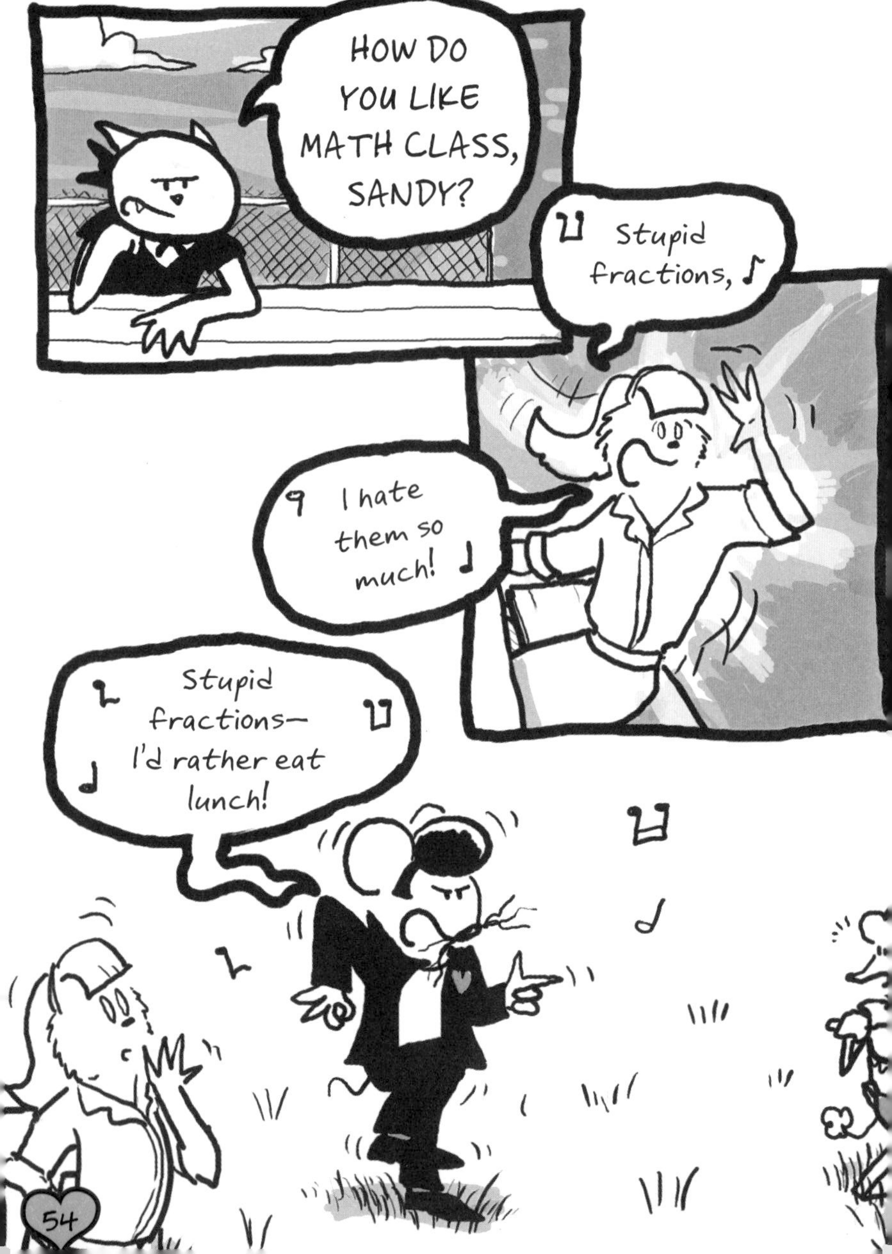
HOW DO YOU LIKE MATH CLASS, SANDY?
Stupid fractions,
I hate them so much!
Stupid fractions— I'd rather eat lunch!

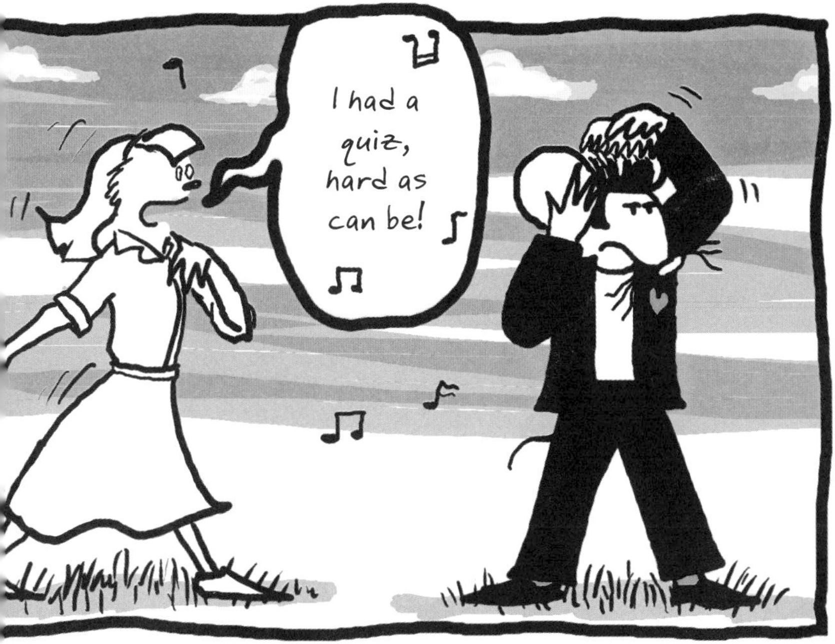
I had a quiz, hard as can be!

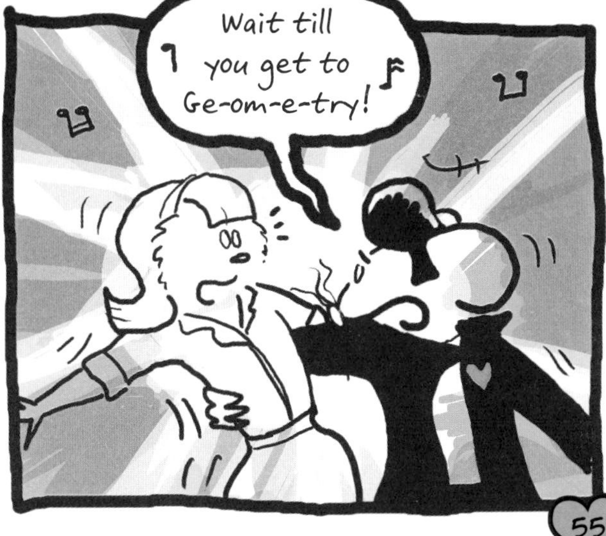
Wait till you get to Ge-om-e-try!

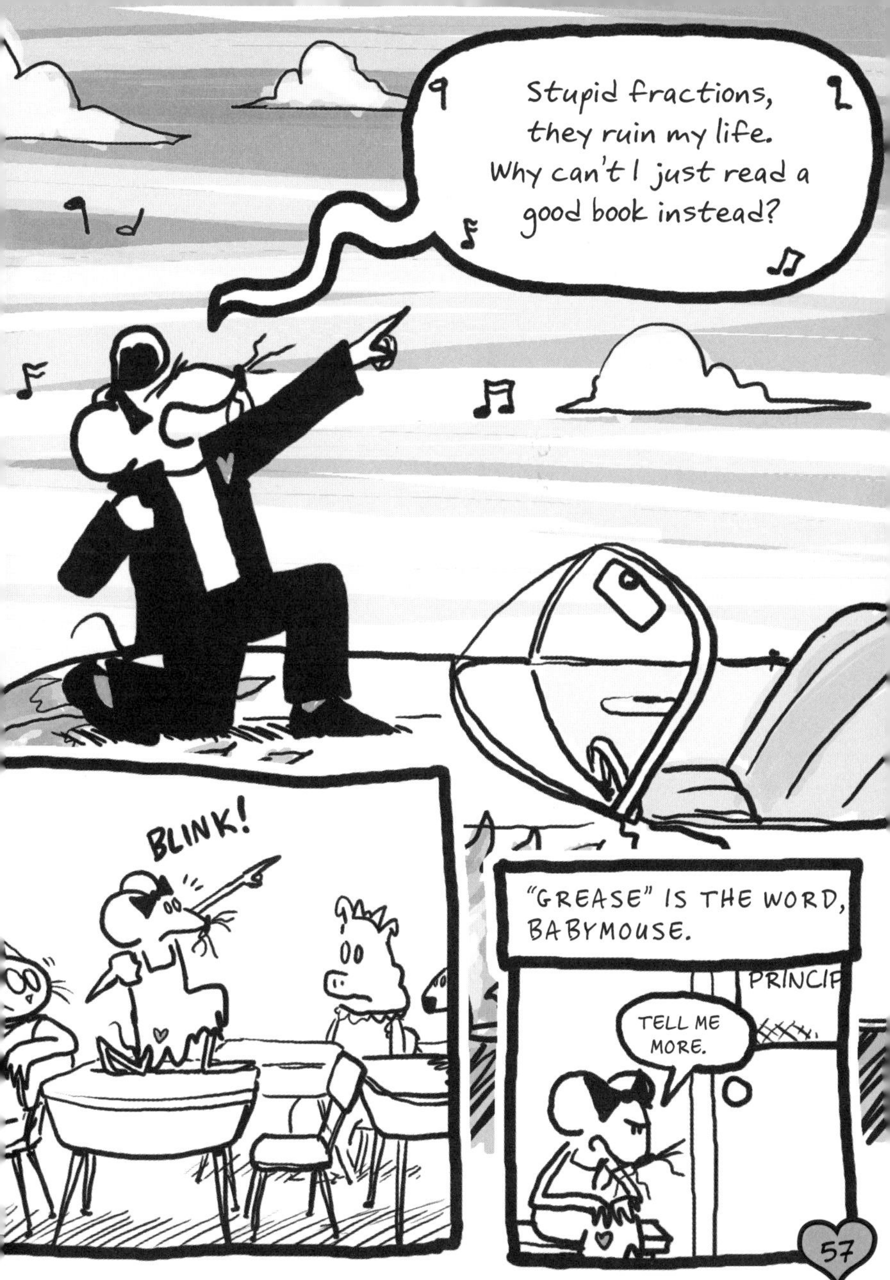
Stupid fractions, they ruin my life. Why can't I just read a good book instead?
BLINK!
"GREASE" IS THE WORD, BABYMOUSE.
PRINCIP
TELL ME MORE.

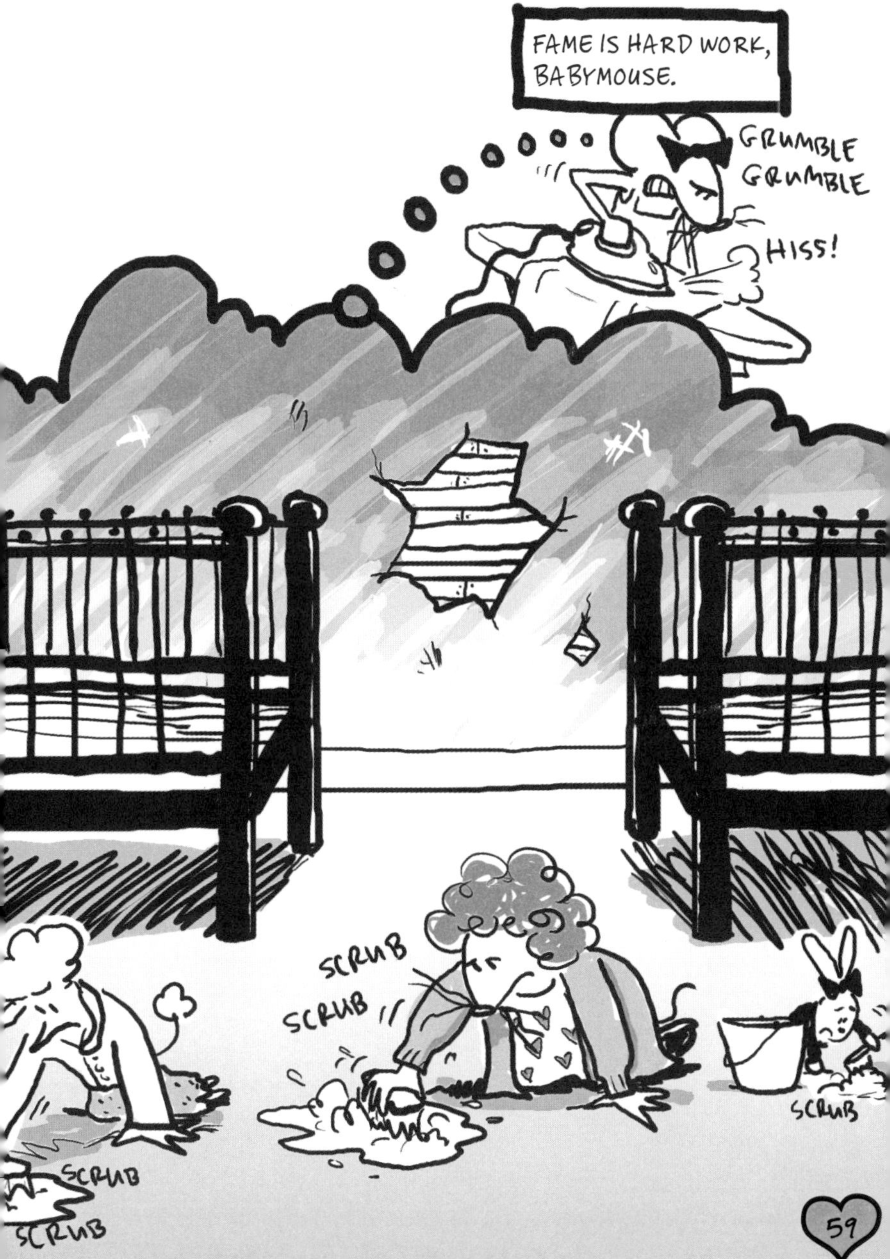
FAME IS HARD WORK, BABYMOUSE.
GRUMBLE GRUMBLE
HISS!
SCRUB
SCRUB
SCRUB
SCRUB
SCRUB

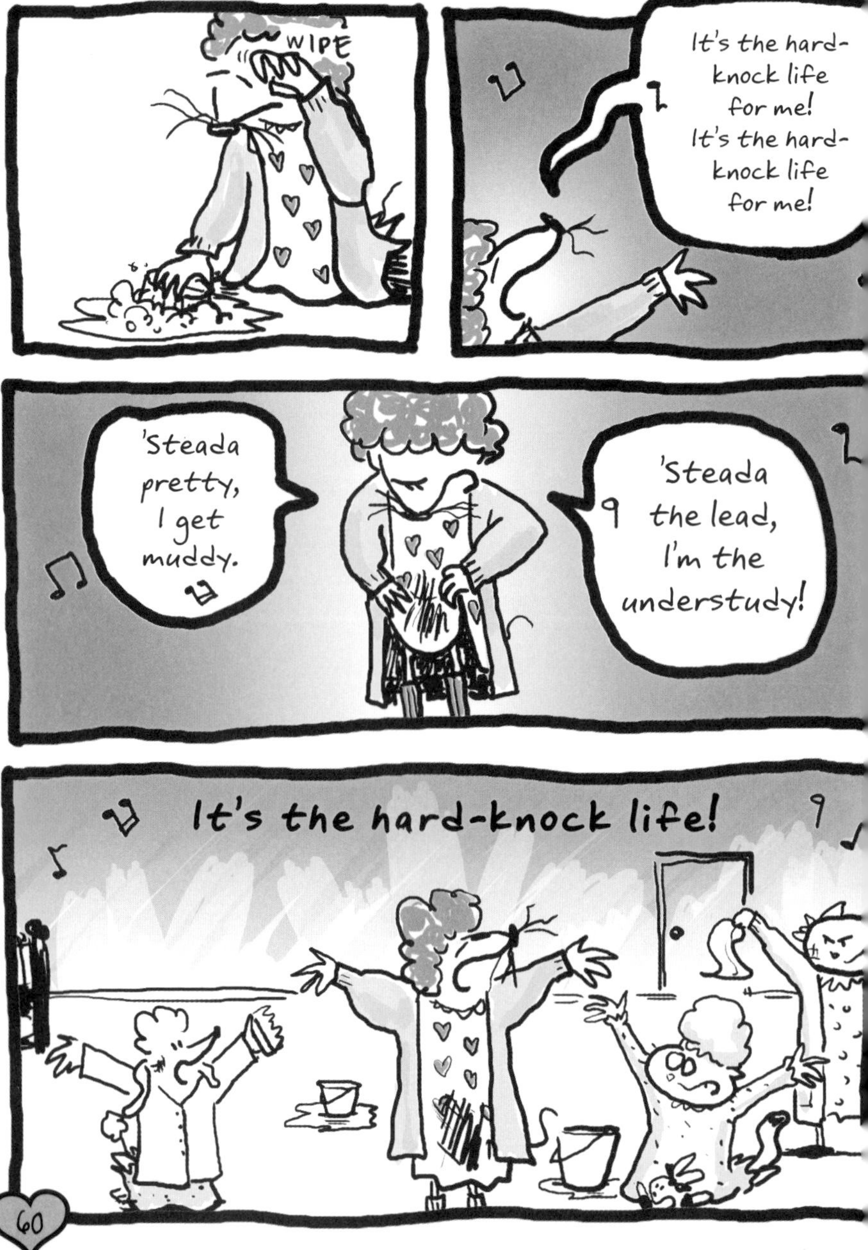
WIPE
It's the hard-knock life for me! It's the hard-knock life for me!
'Steada pretty, I get muddy.
'Steada the lead, I'm the understudy!
It's the hard-knock life!

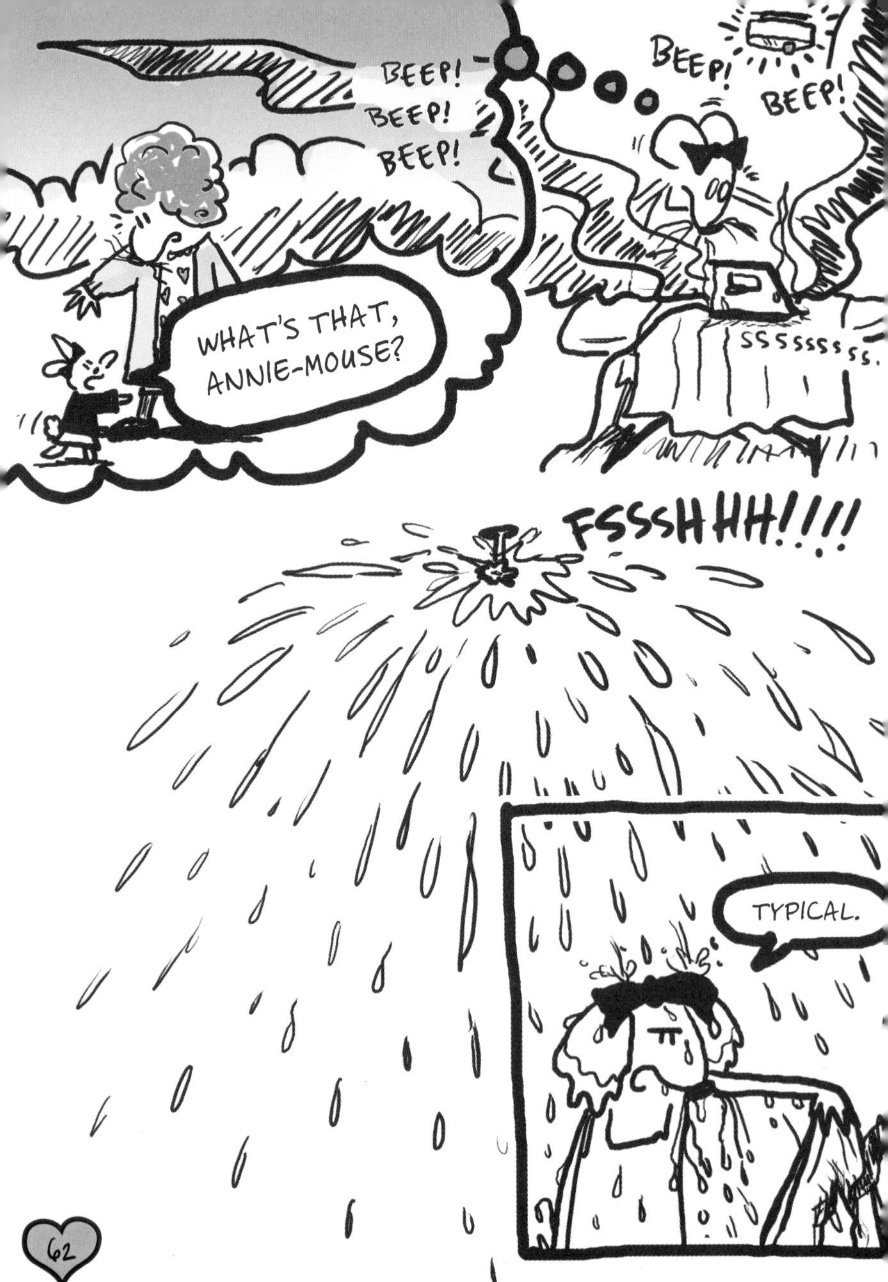
BEEP! BEEP! BEEP!
WHAT'S THAT, ANNIE-MOUSE?
BEEP! BEEP!
SSSSSSSSSS.
FSSSHHH!!!!
TYPICAL.

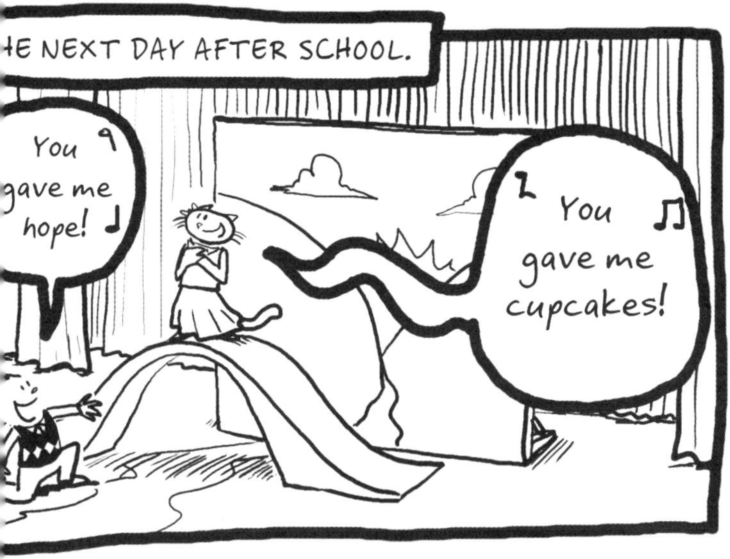
HE NEXT DAY AFTER SCHOOL.
You gave me hope!
You gave me cupcakes!

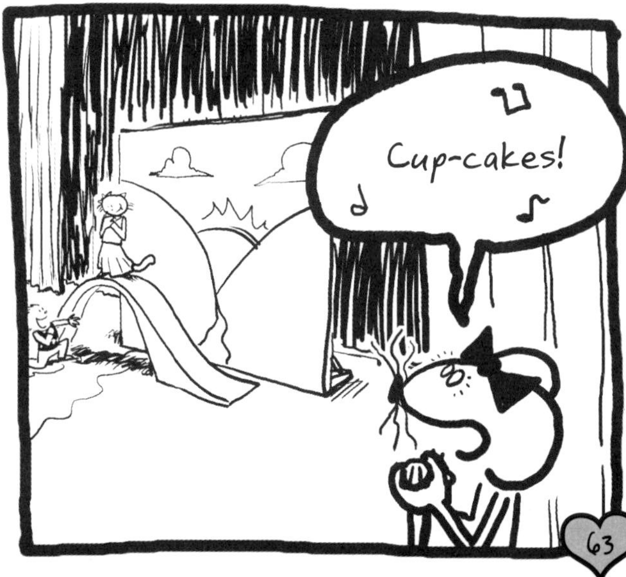
Cup-cakes!

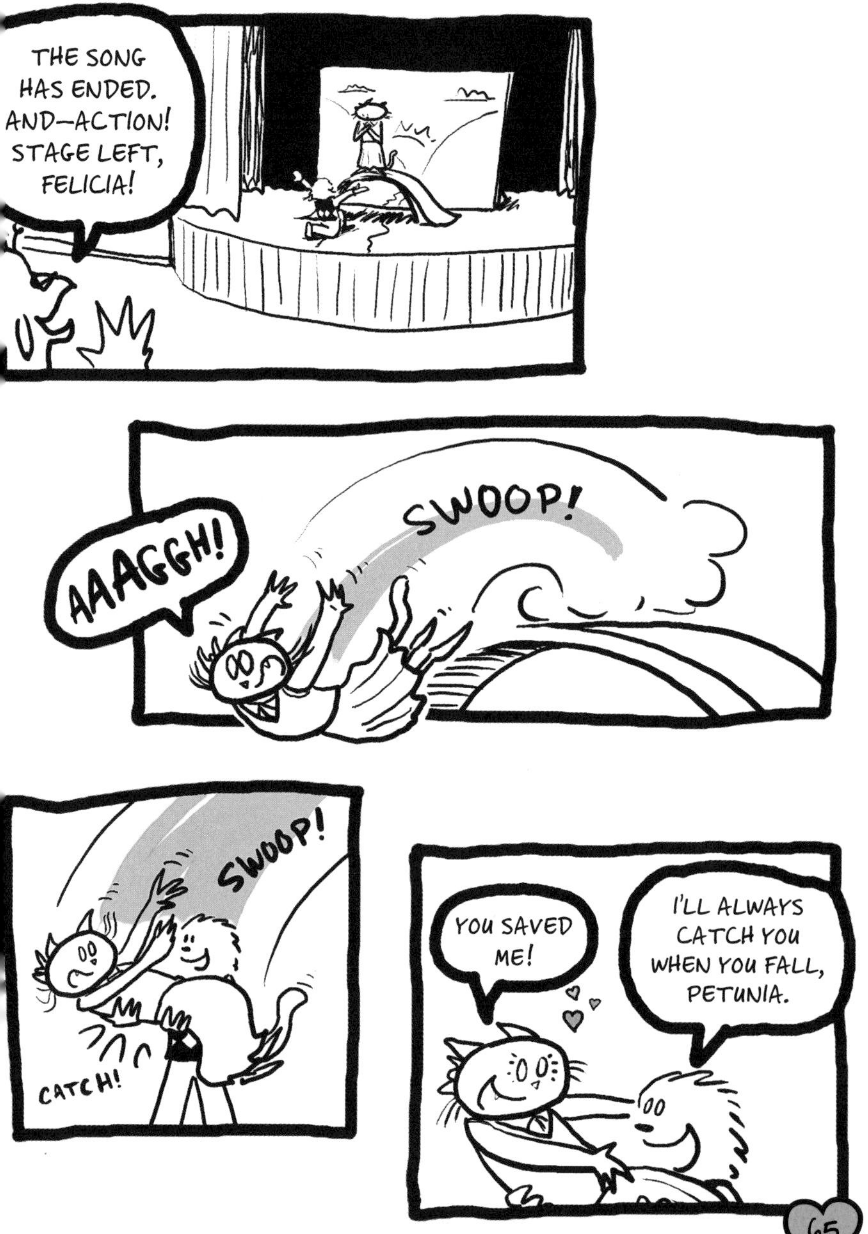
THE SONG HAS ENDED. AND—ACTION! STAGE LEFT, FELICIA!
AAAGGH!
SWOOP!
SWOOP!
CATCH!
YOU SAVED ME!
I'LL ALWAYS CATCH YOU WHEN YOU FALL, PETUNIA.

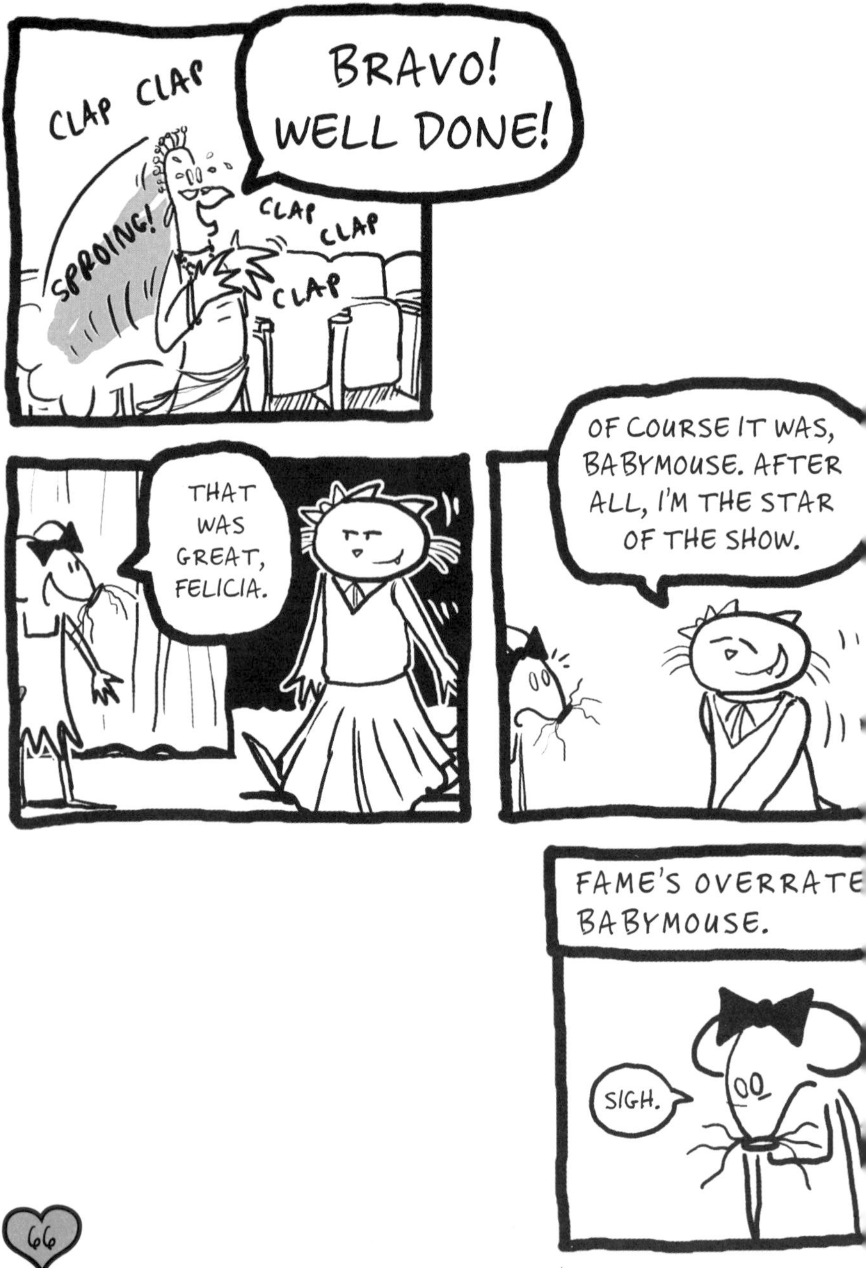
CLAP CLAP
BRAVO! WELL DONE!
SPROING!
CLAP CLAP
CLAP
THAT WAS GREAT, FELICIA.
OF COURSE IT WAS, BABYMOUSE. AFTER ALL, I'M THE STAR OF THE SHOW.
FAME'S OVERRATE
BABYMOUSE.
SIGH.

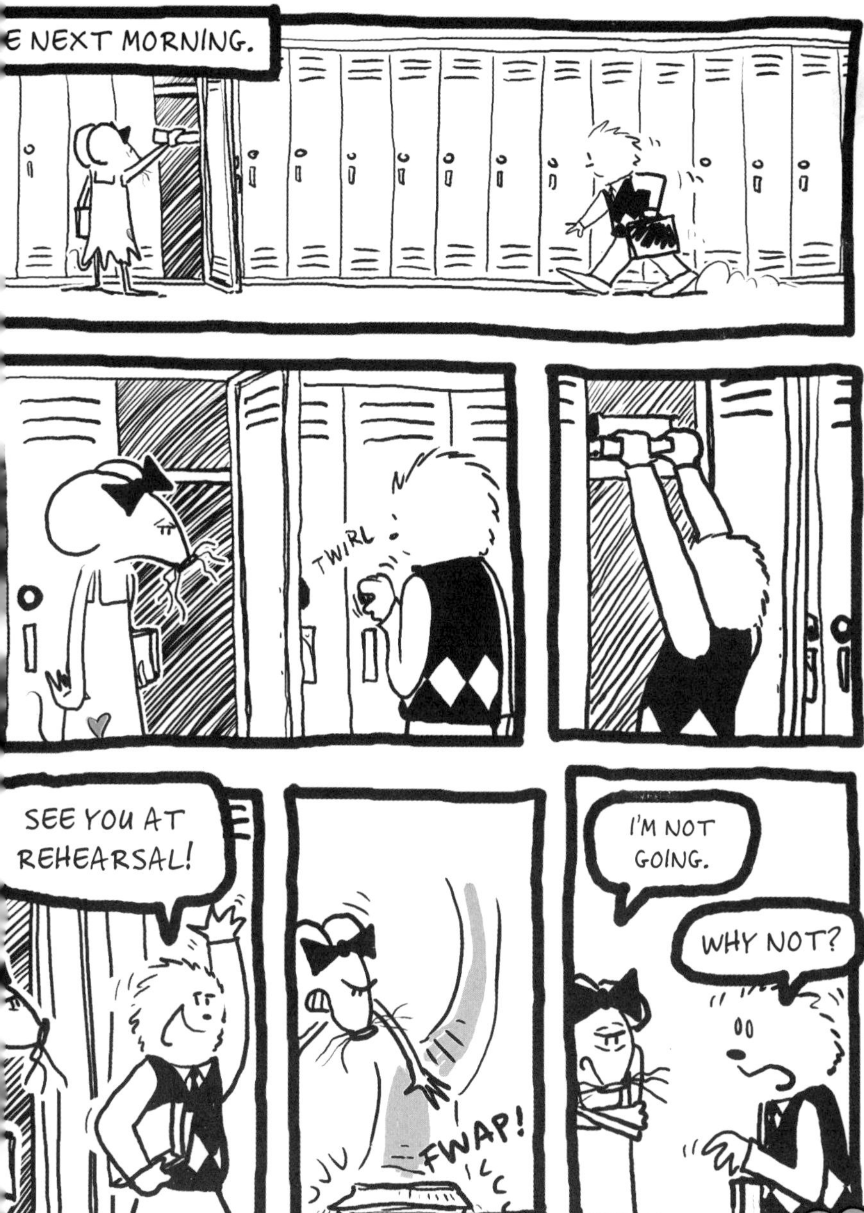
E NEXT MORNING.
TWIRL
SEE YOU AT REHEARSAL!
FWAP!
I'M NOT GOING.
WHY NOT?

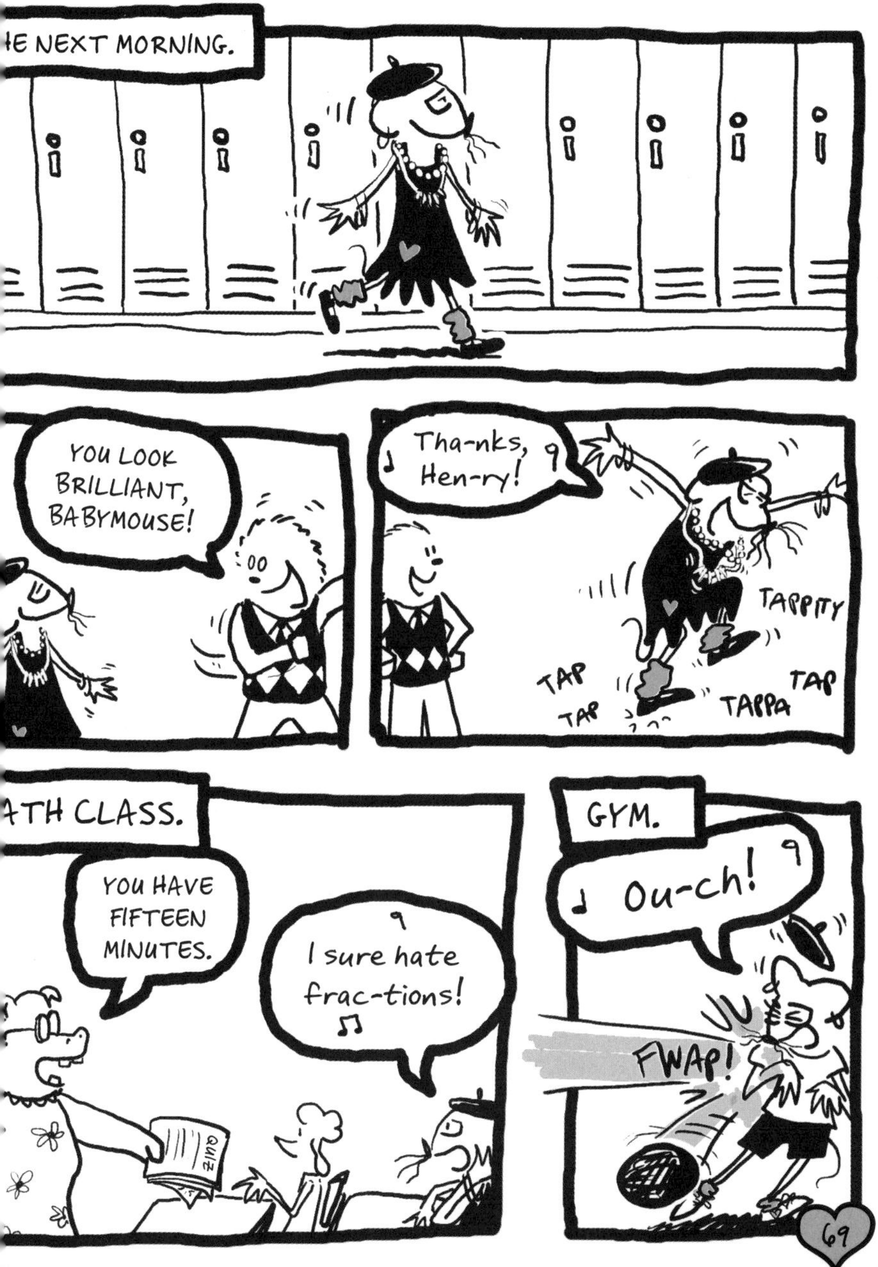

HE NEXT MORNING.
YOU LOOK BRILLIANT, BABYMOUSE!
Tha-nks, Hen-ry!
TAPPITY
TAP
TAP
TAP
TAPPA
ATH CLASS.
YOU HAVE FIFTEEN MINUTES.
QUIZ
I sure hate frac-tions!
GYM.
Ou-ch!
FWAP!

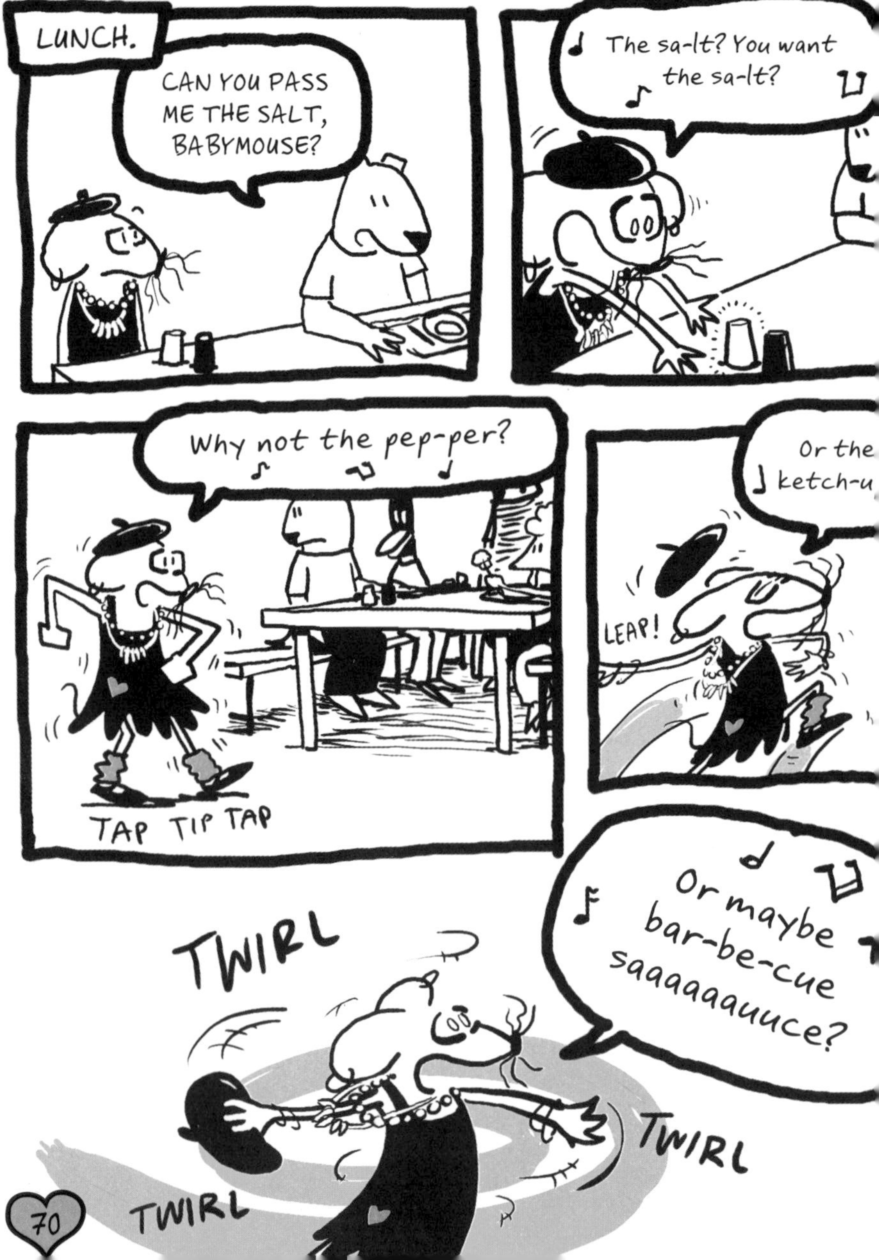

LUNCH.
CAN YOU PASS ME THE SALT, BABYMOUSE?
The sa-lt? You want the sa-lt?
Why not the pep-per?
TAP TIP TAP
Or the
ketch-u
LEAP!
TWIRL
Or maybe bar-be-cue saaaaaauuce?
TWIRL
TWIRL

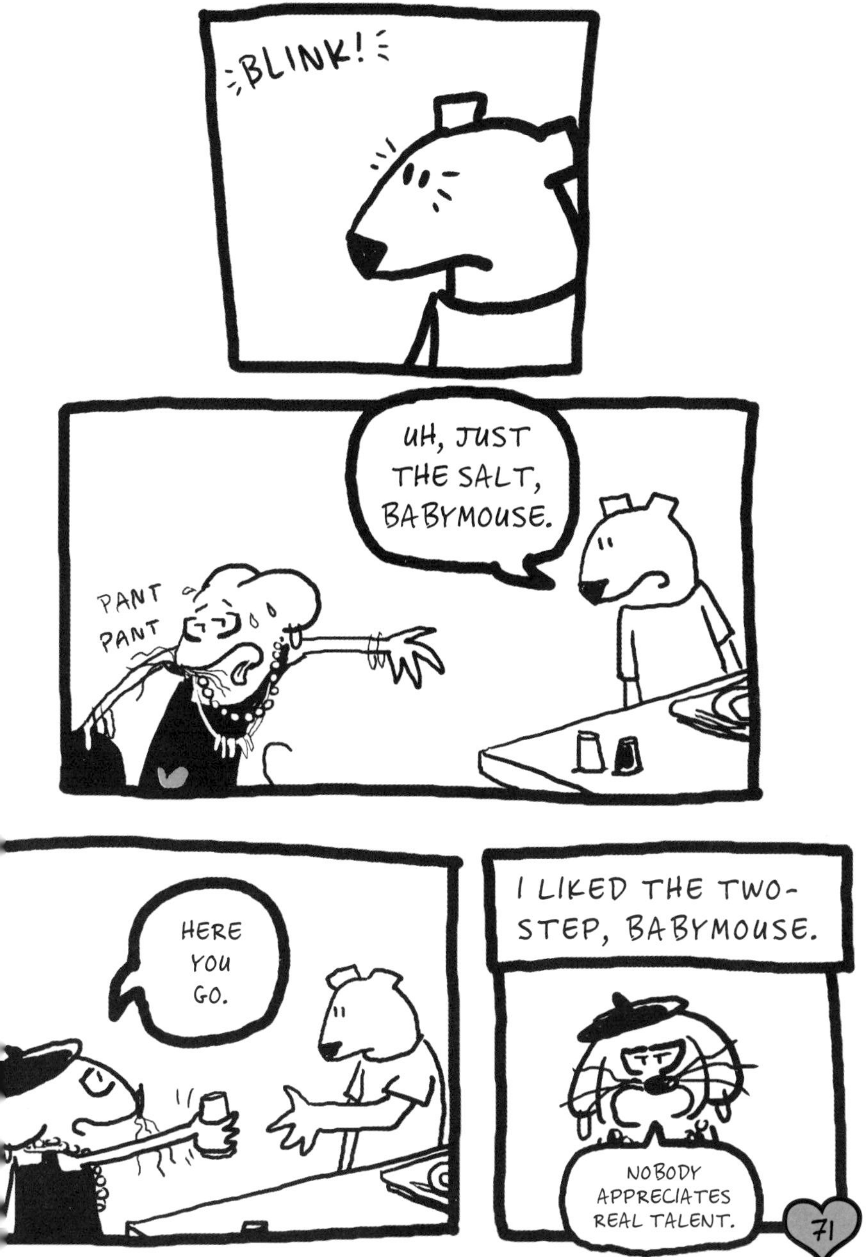
BLINK!
UH, JUST THE SALT, BABYMOUSE.
PANT PANT
HERE YOU GO.
I LIKED THE TWO-STEP, BABYMOUSE.
NOBODY APPRECIATES REAL TALENT.

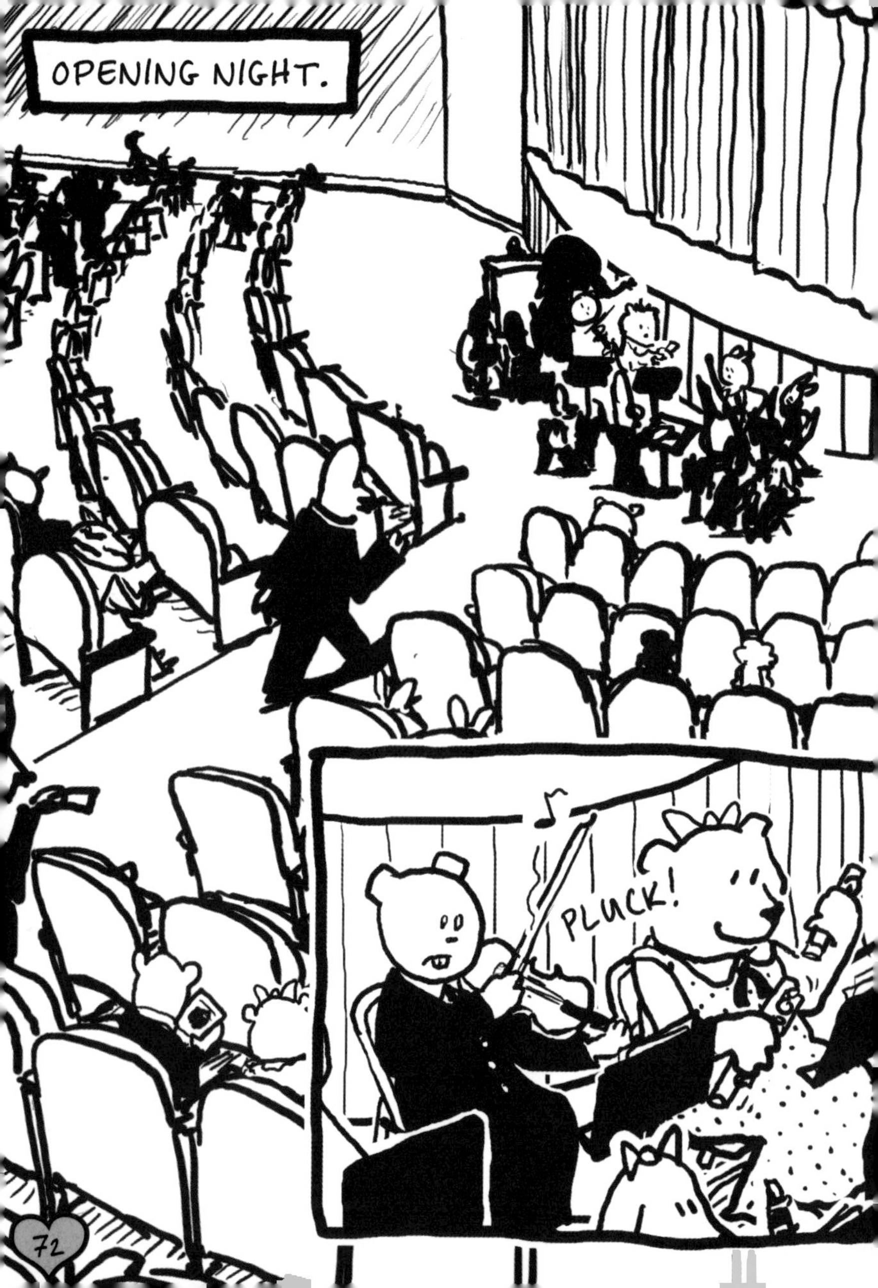
OPENING NIGHT.
PLUCK!

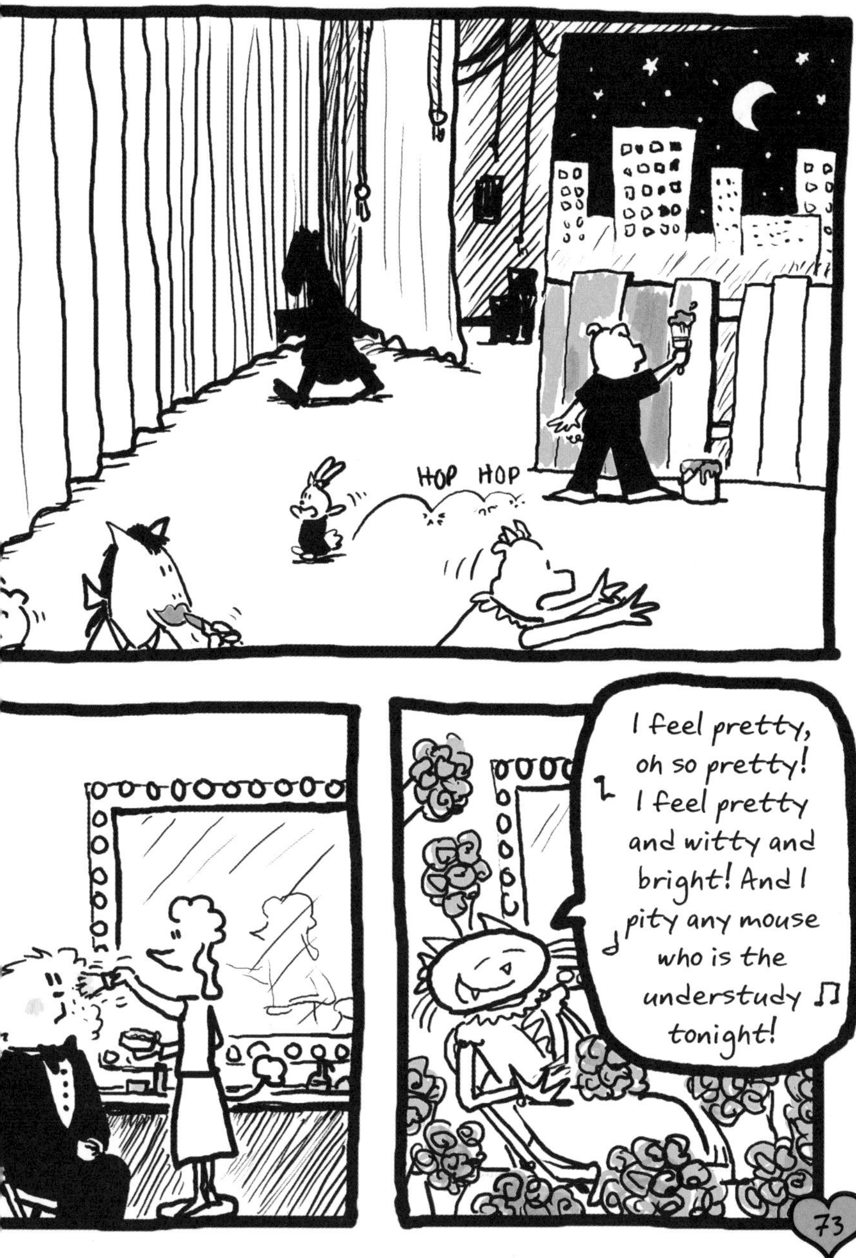
HOP HOP
I feel pretty, oh so pretty! I feel pretty and witty and bright! And I pity any mouse who is the understudy tonight!

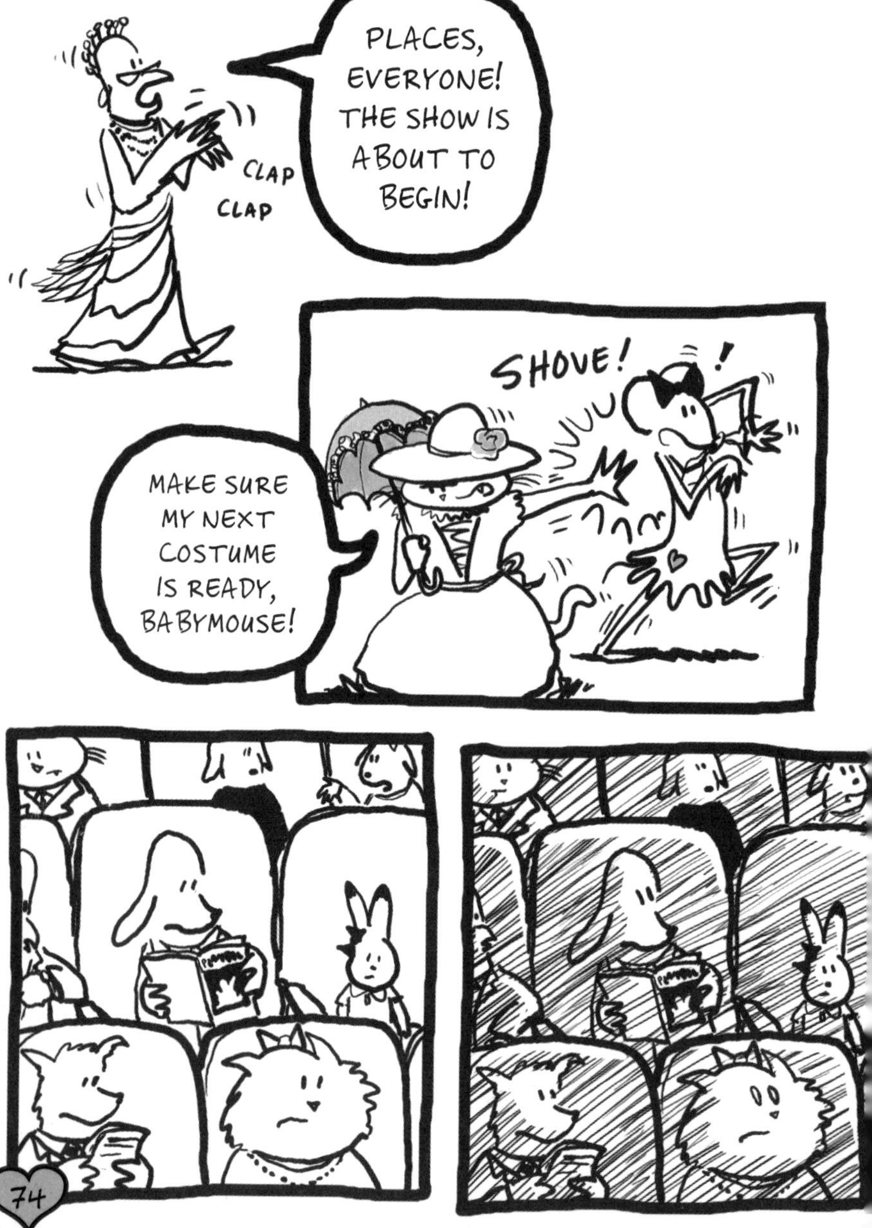
PLACES, EVERYONE! THE SHOW IS ABOUT TO BEGIN!
CLAP
CLAP
SHOVE!
MAKE SURE MY NEXT COSTUME IS READY, BABYMOUSE!

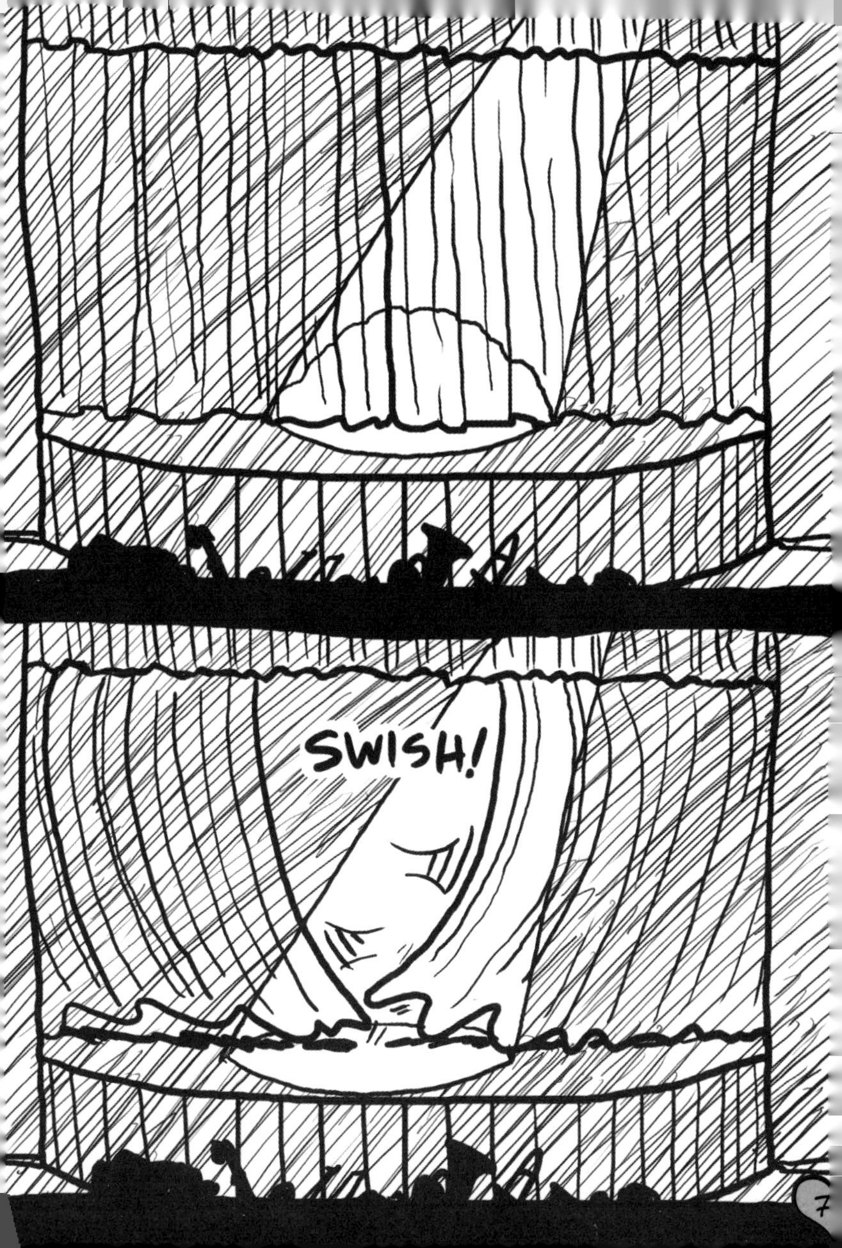
SWISH!

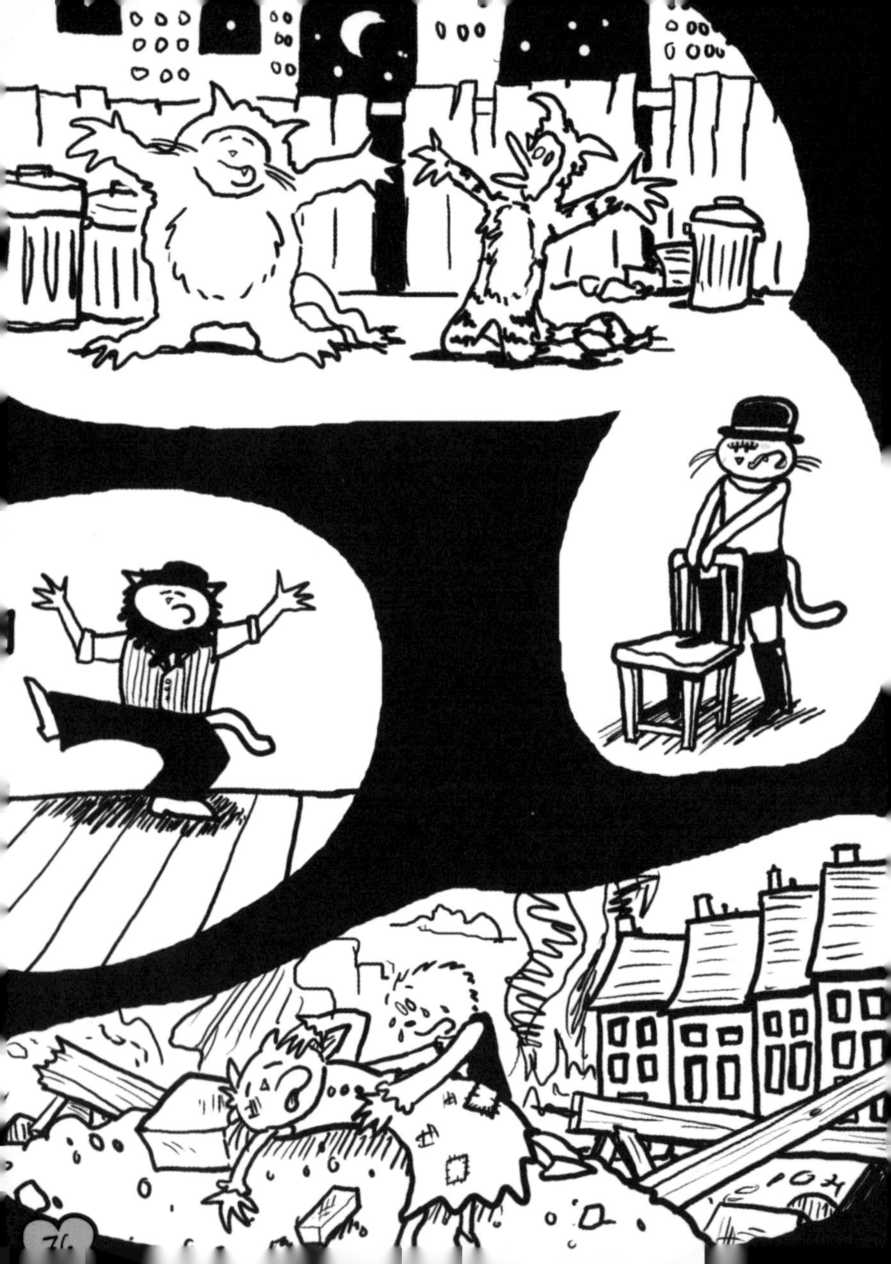

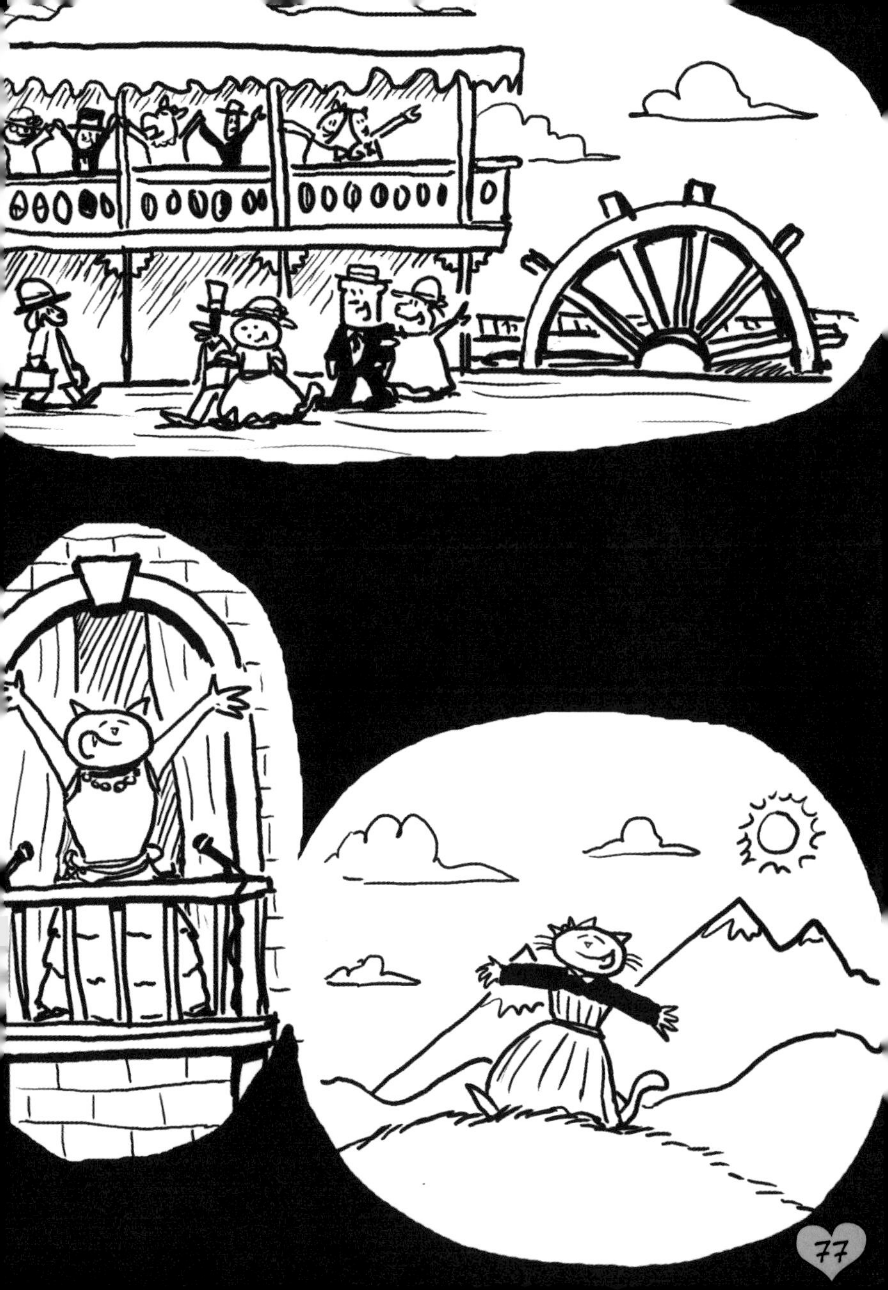
PGH

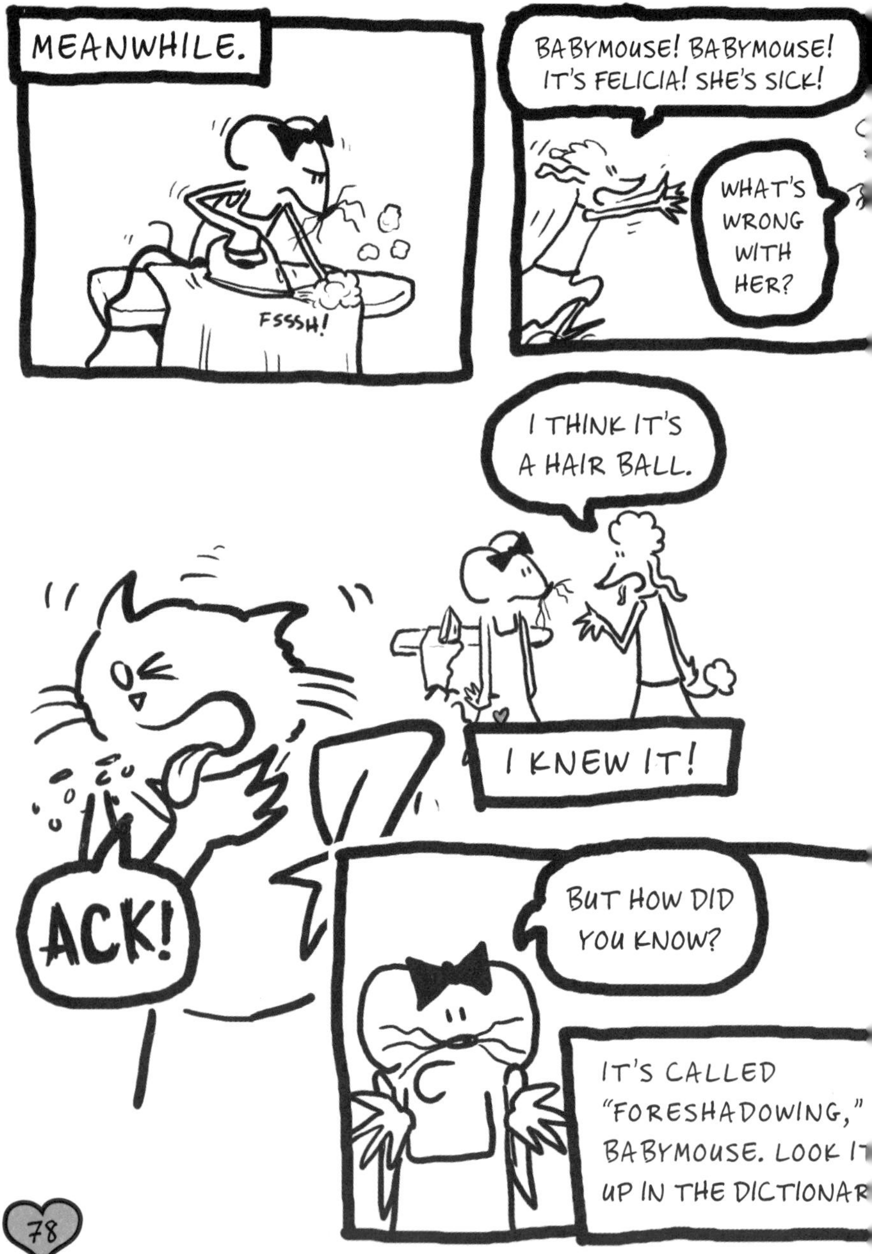
MEANWHILE.
FSSSH!
BABYMOUSE! BABYMOUSE! IT'S FELICIA! SHE'S SICK!
WHAT'S WRONG WITH HER?
I THINK IT'S A HAIR BALL.
ACK!
I KNEW IT!
BUT HOW DID YOU KNOW?
IT'S CALLED "FORESHADOWING," BABYMOUSE. LOOK IT UP IN THE DICTIONAR

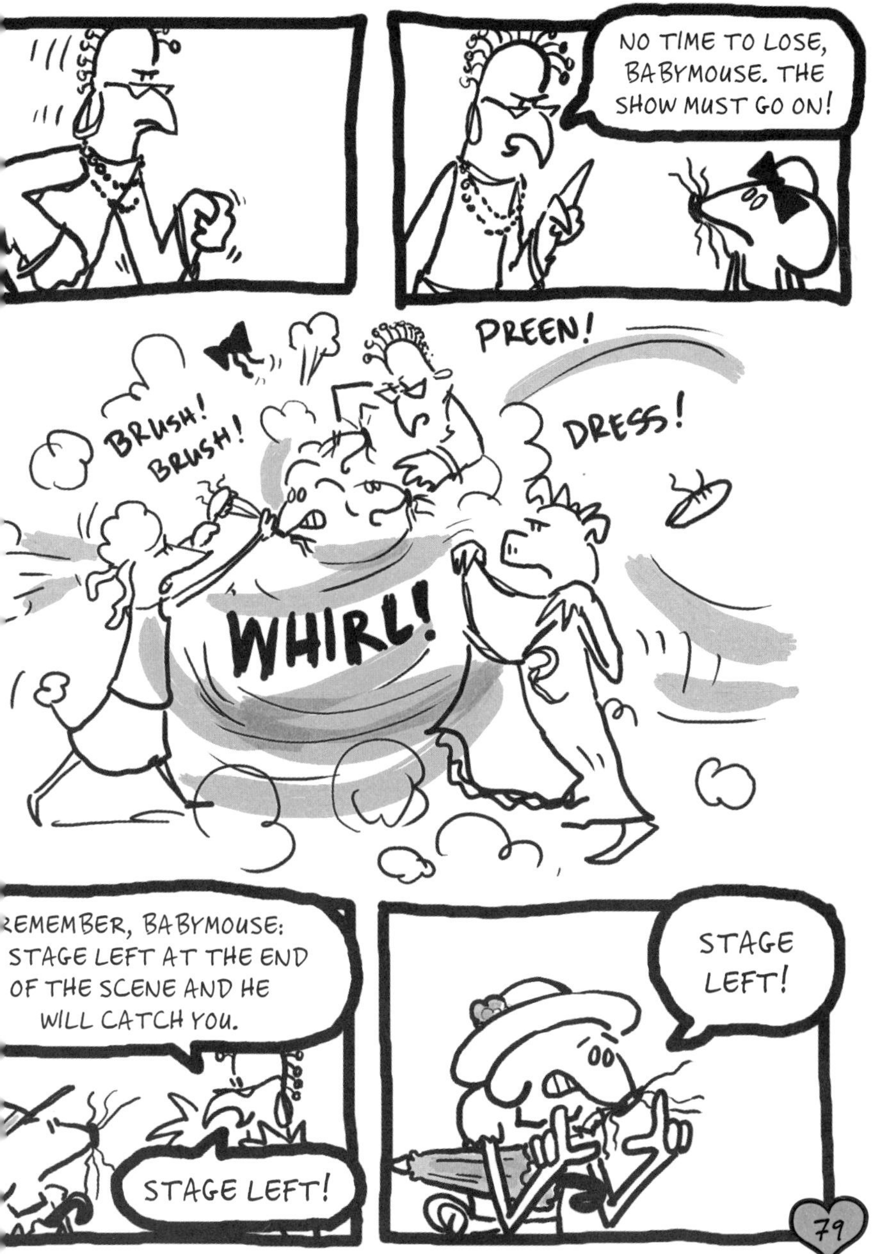
NO TIME TO LOSE, BABYMOUSE. THE SHOW MUST GO ON!
PREEN!
BRUSH! BRUSH!
DRESS!
WHIRL!
REMEMBER, BABYMOUSE: STAGE LEFT AT THE END OF THE SCENE AND HE WILL CATCH YOU.
STAGE LEFT!
STAGE LEFT!

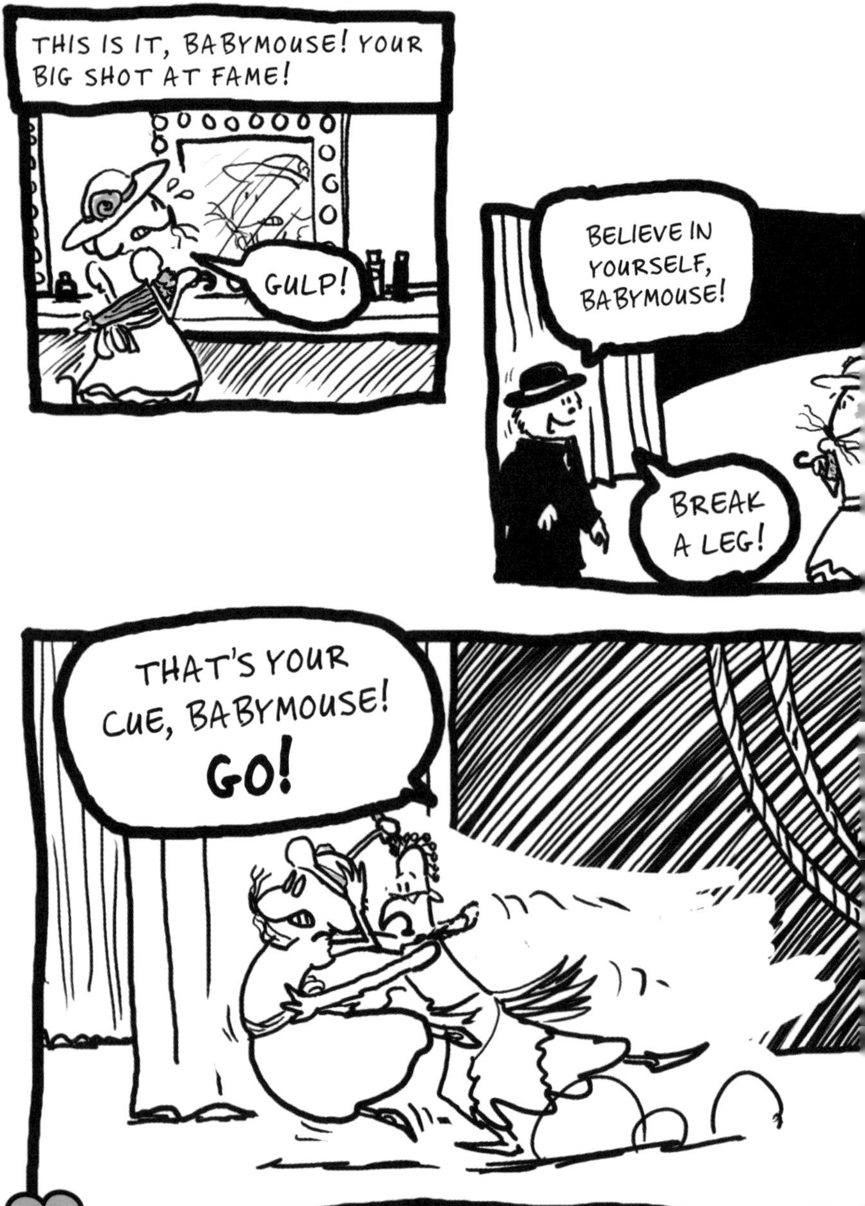
THIS IS IT, BABYMOUSE! YOUR BIG SHOT AT FAME!
GULP!
BELIEVE IN YOURSELF, BABYMOUSE!
BREAK A LEG!
THAT'S YOUR CUE, BABYMOUSE! GO!

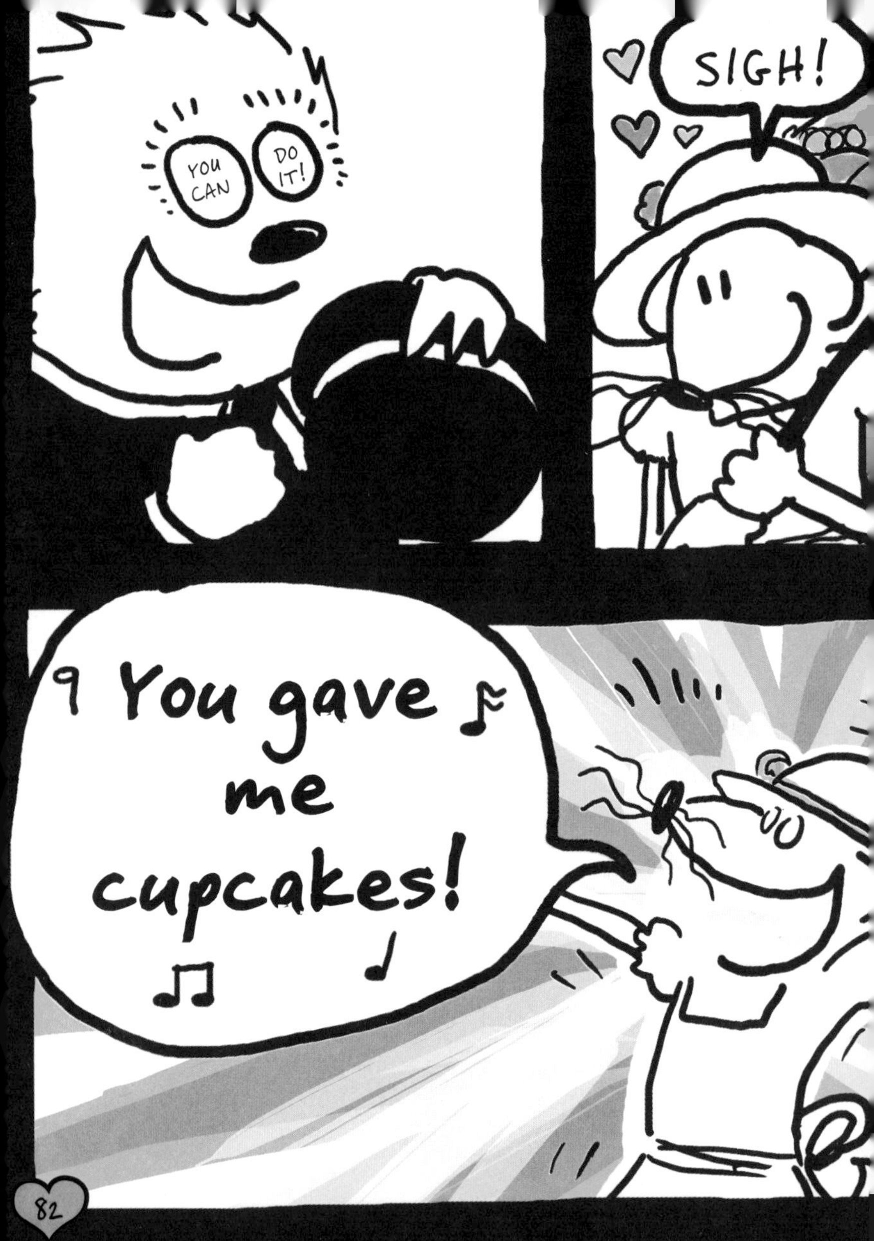
YOU CAN DO IT!
SIGH!
You gave me cupcakes!

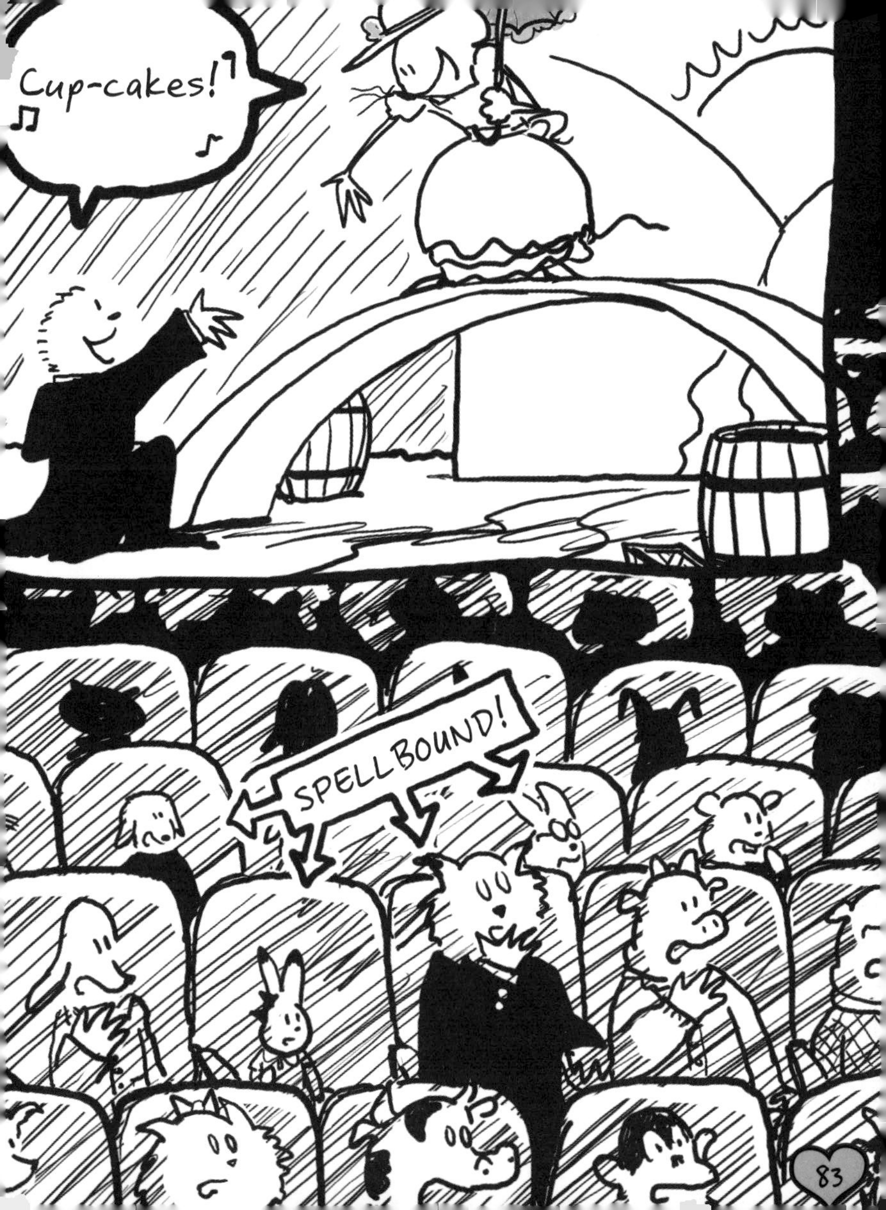
Cup-cakes!
SPELLBOUND!

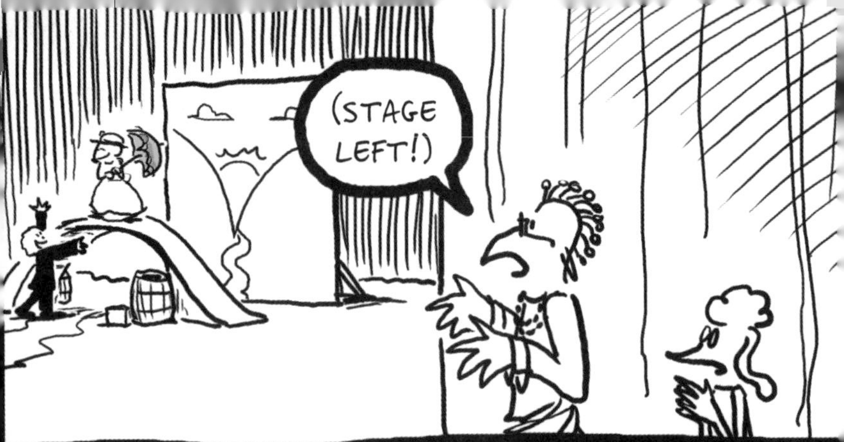
(STAGE LEFT!)

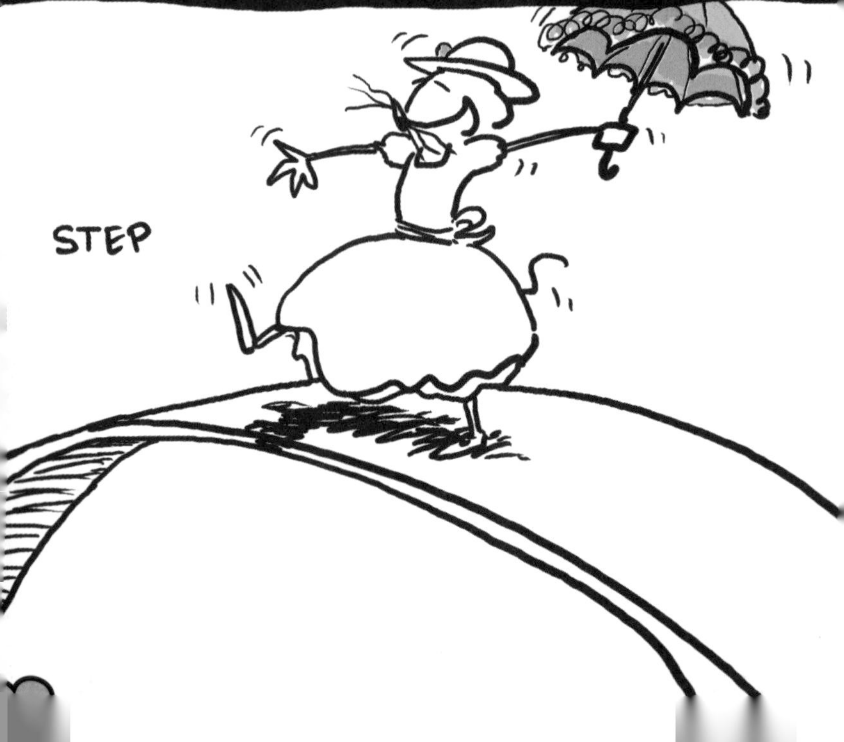
STEP

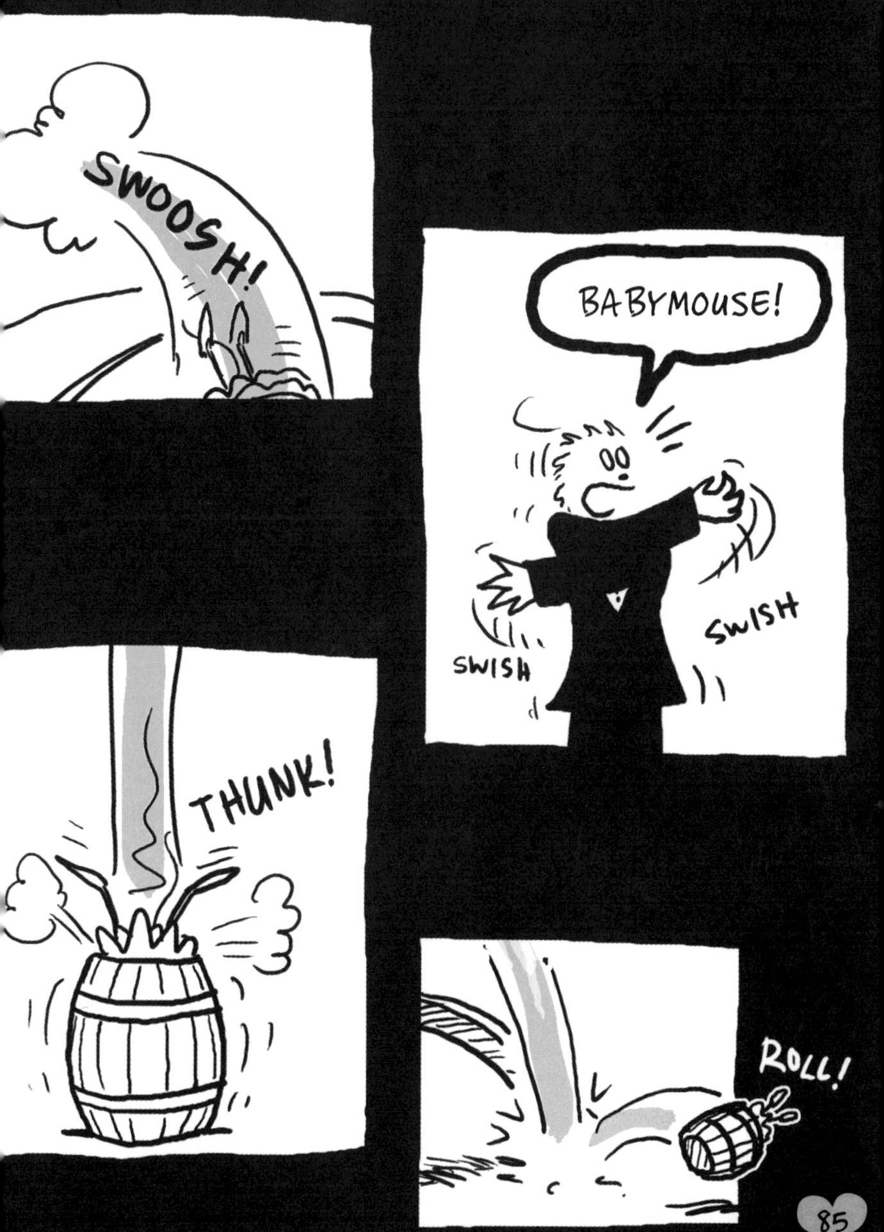
SWOOSH!
BABYMOUSE!
SWISH
SWISH
THUNK!
ROLL!

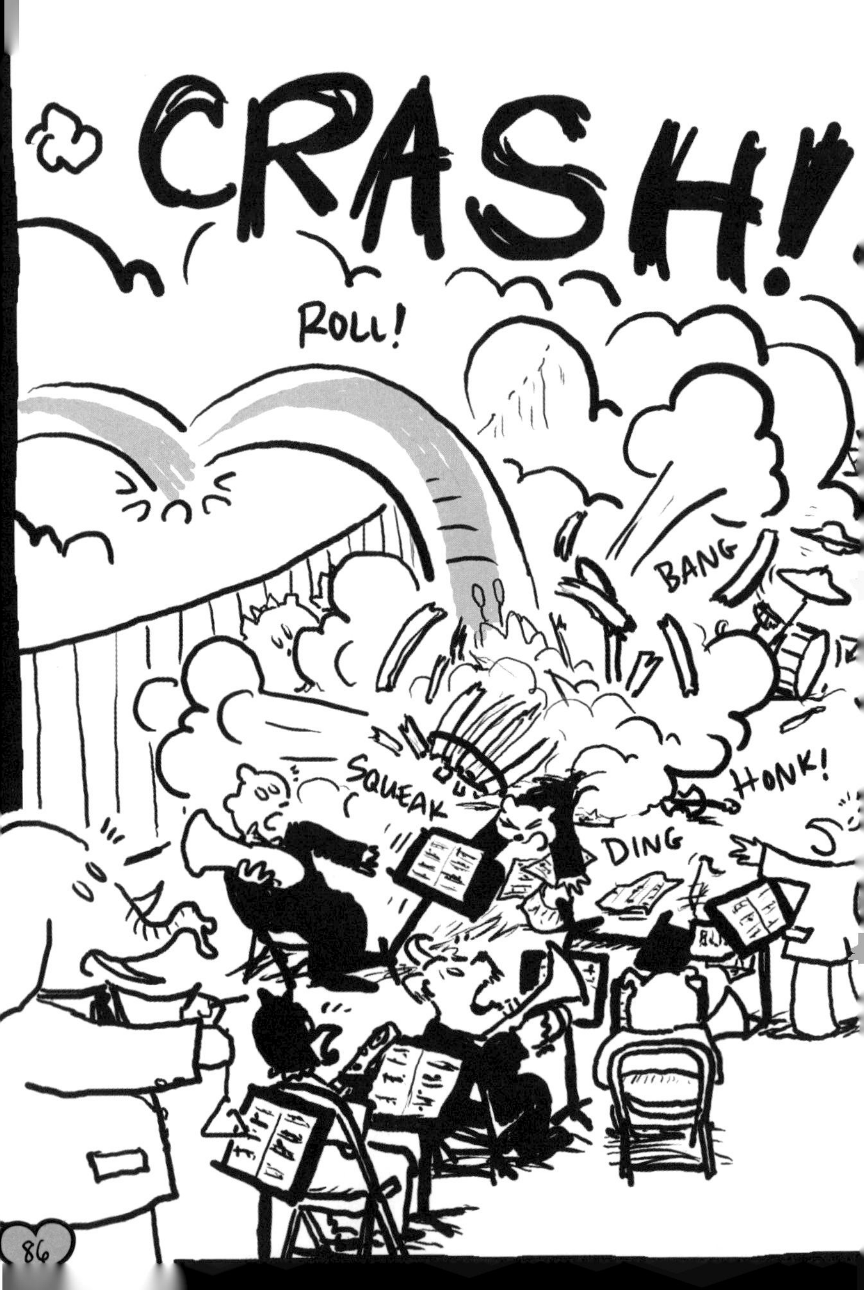
CRASH!
ROLL!
BANG
SQUEAK
HONK!
DING

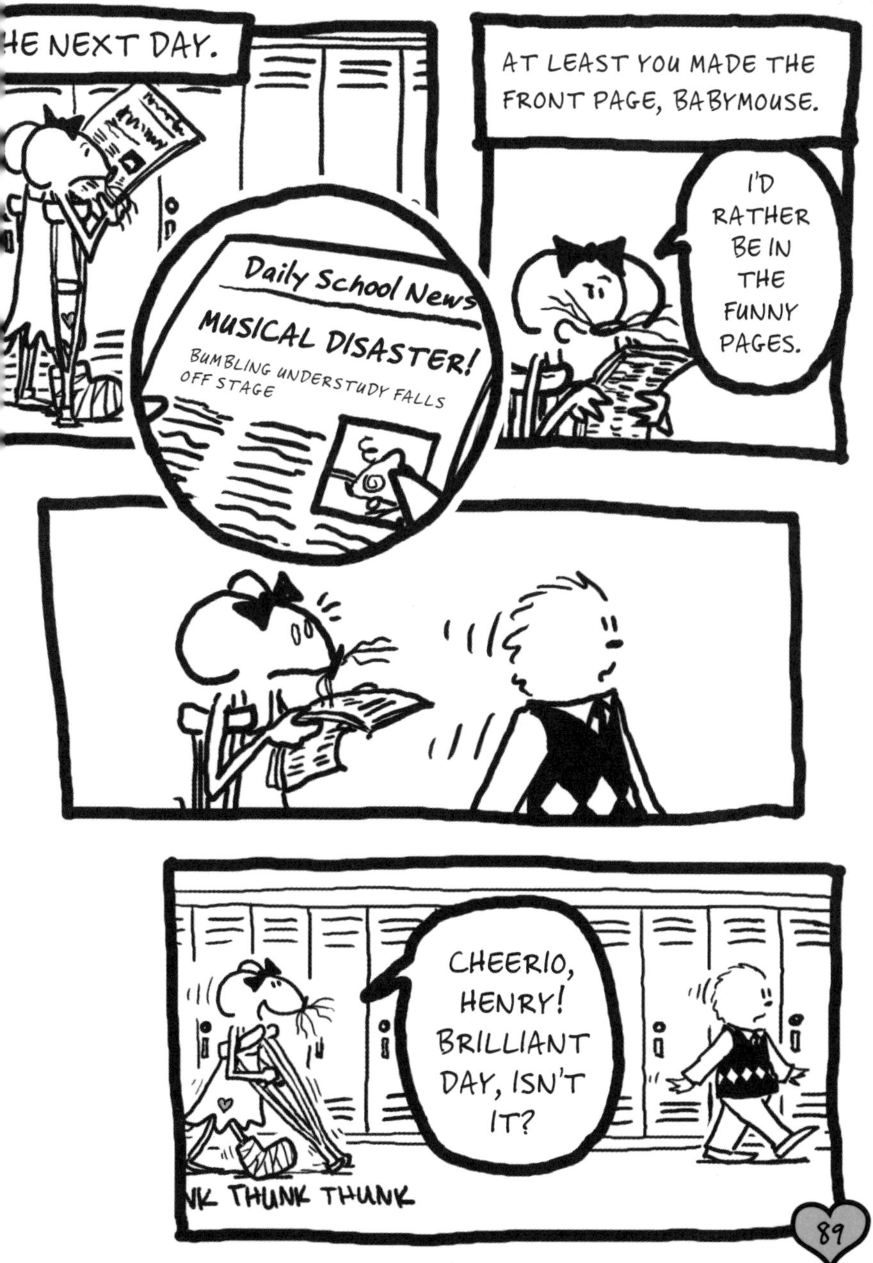

HE NEXT DAY.
Daily School News
MUSICAL DISASTER!
BUMBLING UNDERSTUDY FALLS OFF STAGE
AT LEAST YOU MADE THE FRONT PAGE, BABYMOUSE.
I'D RATHER BE IN THE FUNNY PAGES.
CHEERIO, HENRY! BRILLIANT DAY, ISN'T IT?
NK THUNK THUNK

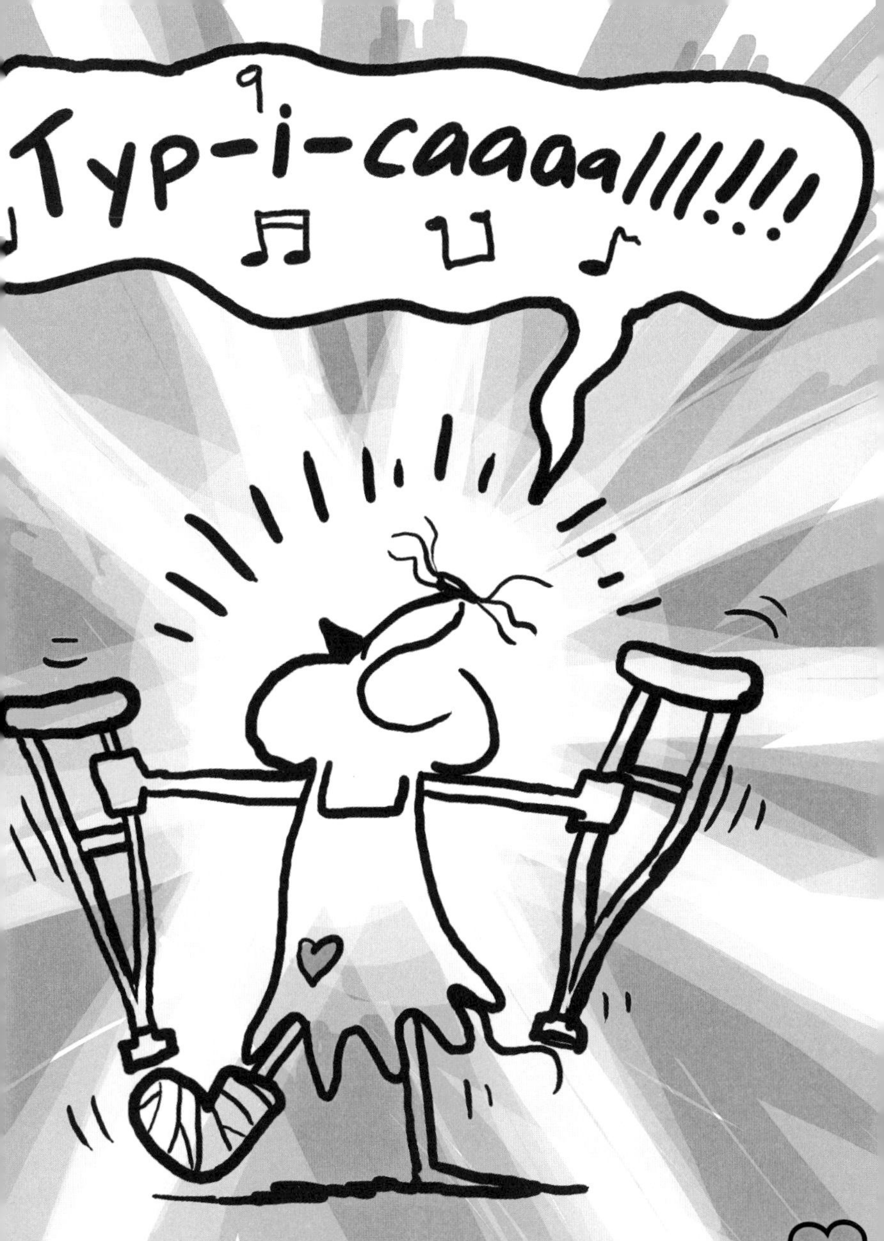
Typ-i-caaaal!!!!!!

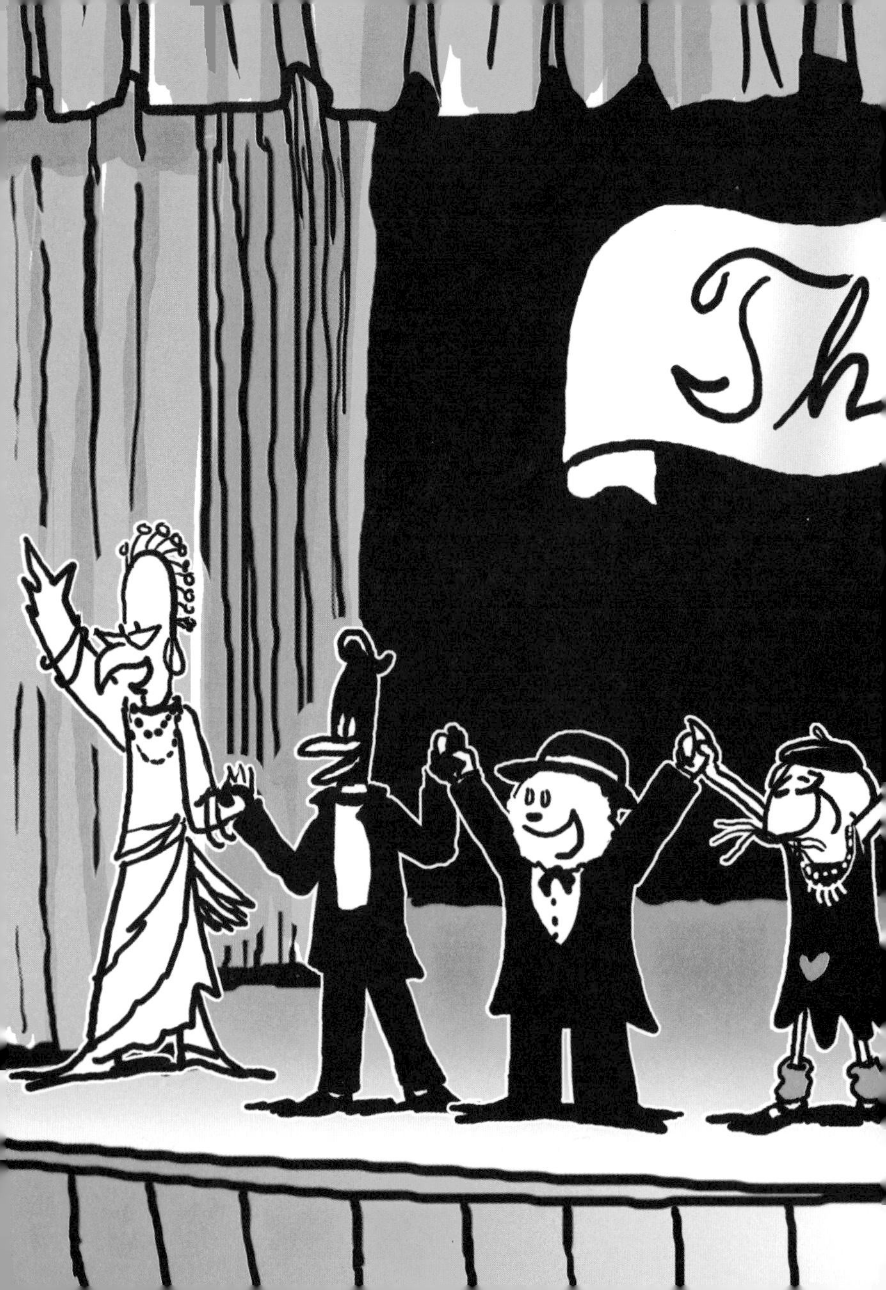
Th

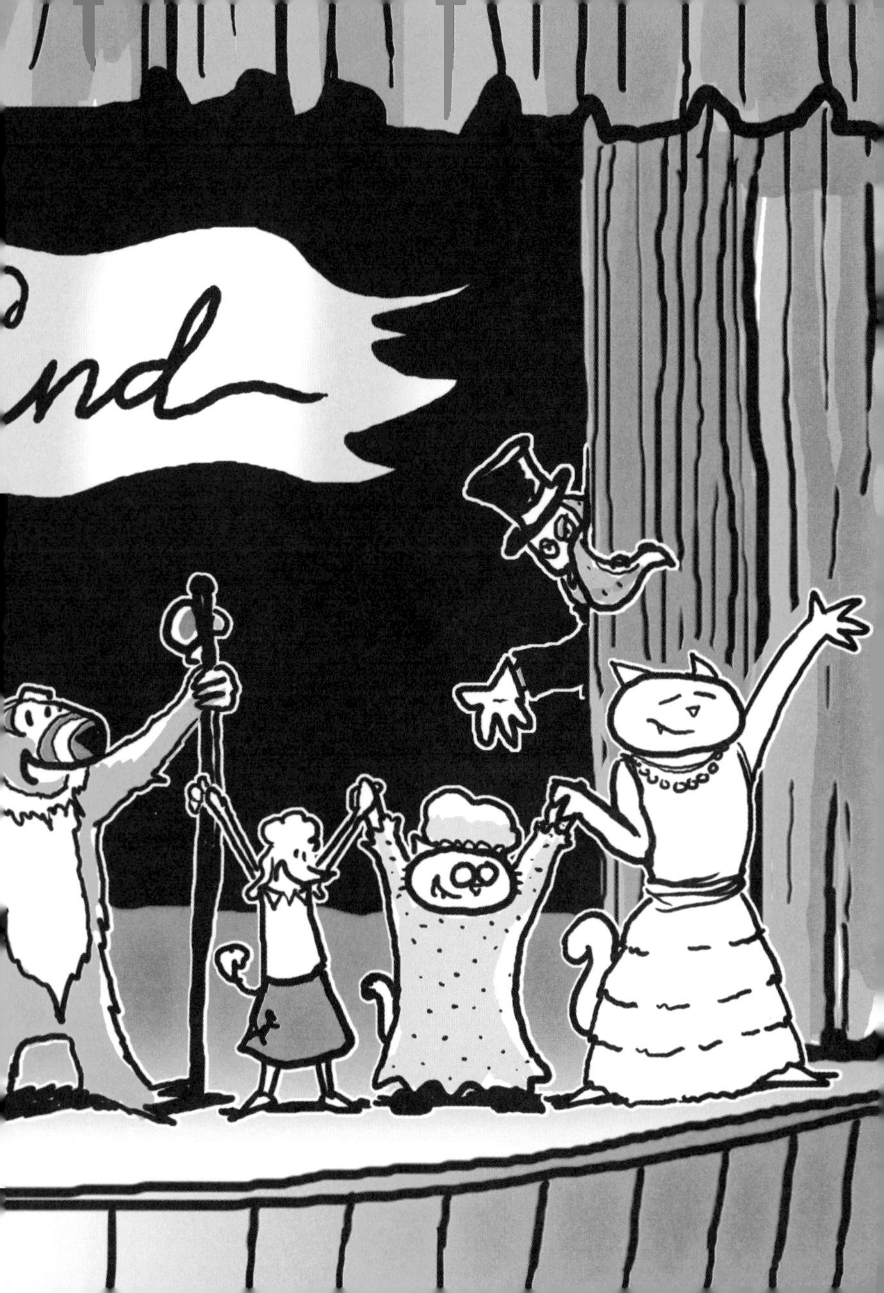
nd

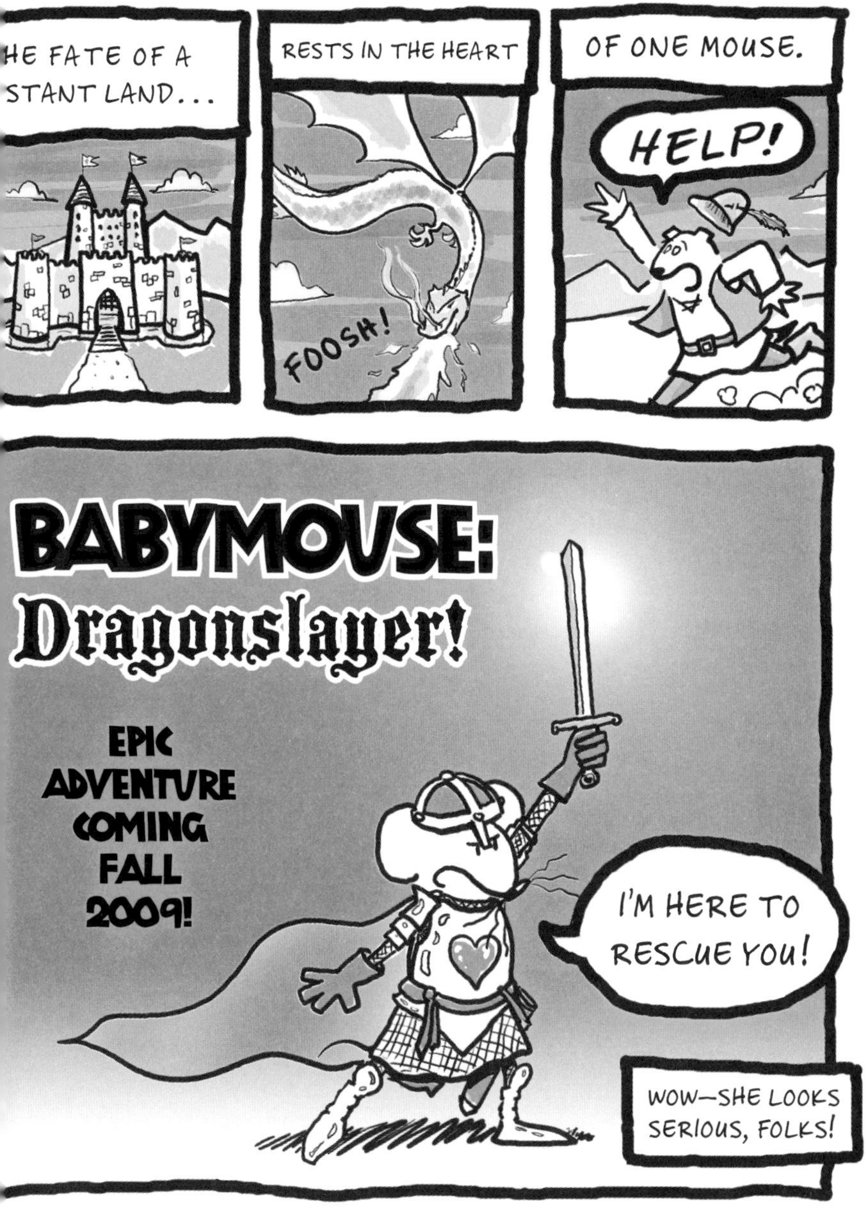
HE FATE OF A
STANT LAND...
RESTS IN THE HEART
OF ONE MOUSE.
FOOSH!
HELP!
BABYMOUSE:
Dragonslayer!
EPIC ADVENTURE COMING FALL 2009!
I'M HERE TO RESCUE YOU!
WOW—SHE LOOKS SERIOUS, FOLKS!

# BABYMOUSE

## CAPTION CONTEST WINNER!

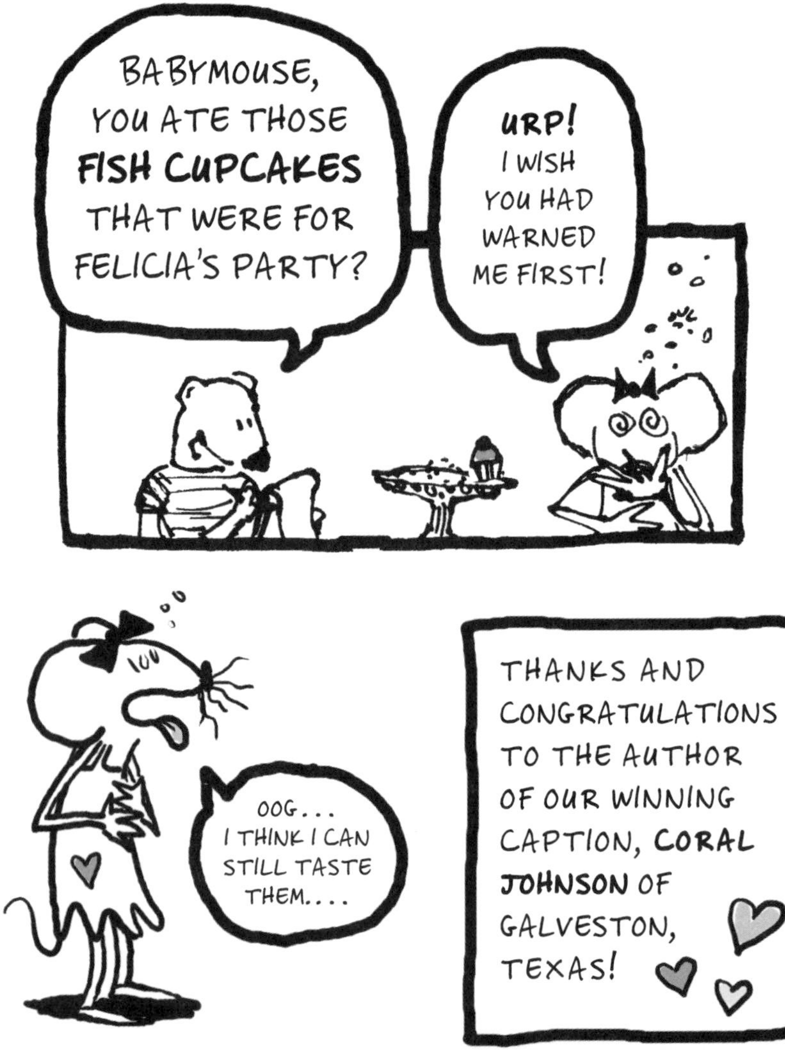

BABYMOUSE, YOU ATE THOSE **FISH CUPCAKES** THAT WERE FOR FELICIA'S PARTY?
**URP!** I WISH YOU HAD WARNED ME FIRST!
OOG... I THINK I CAN STILL TASTE THEM....
THANKS AND CONGRATULATIONS TO THE AUTHOR OF OUR WINNING CAPTION, **CORAL JOHNSON** OF GALVESTON, TEXAS!